PENGUIN PO

KIN
BY WILLIAM SHAKESPEARE

PENGUIN POPULAR CLASSICS

KING LEAR

WILLIAM SHAKESPEARE

PENGUIN BOOKS

PENGUIN BOOKS

Published by the Penguin Group
Penguin Books Ltd, 80 Strand, London WC2R ORL, England
Penguin Putnam Inc., 375 Hudson Street, New York, New York 10014, USA
Penguin Books Australia Ltd, Ringwood, Victoria, Australia
Penguin Books Canada Ltd, 10 Alcorn Avenue, Toronto, Ontario, Canada M4V 3B2
Penguin Books India (P) Ltd, 11 Community Centre, Panchsheel Park,
New Delhi — 110 017, India
Penguin Books (NZ) Ltd, Cnr Rosedale and Airborne Roads, Albany, Auckland,
New Zealand
Penguin Books (South Africa) (Pty) Ltd, 24 Sturdee Avenue, Rosebank 2196, South Africa

Penguin Books Ltd, Registered Offices: 80 Strand, London WC2R ORL, England

www.penguin.com

Published in Penguin Popular Classics 1994
1

Copyright 1937, 1949 by the Estate of G. B. Harrison

Printed in the UK by CPI Bookmarque, Croydon, CR0 4TD

ISBN 978-0-14062-381-9

WILLIAM SHAKESPEARE

William Shakespeare was born at Stratford upon Avon in April, 1564. He was the third child, and eldest son, of John Shakespeare and Mary Arden. His father was one of the most prosperous men of Stratford, who held in turn the chief offices in the town. His mother was of gentle birth, the daughter of Robert Arden of Wilmcote. In December, 1582, Shakespeare married Ann Hathaway, daughter of a farmer of Shottery, near Stratford; their first child Susanna was baptized on May 6, 1583, and twins, Hamnet and Judith, on February 22, 1585. Little is known of Shakespeare's early life; but it is unlikely that a writer who dramatized such an incomparable range and variety of human kinds and experiences should have spent his early manhood entirely in placid pursuits in a country town. There is one tradition, not universally accepted, that he fled from Stratford because he was in trouble for deer stealing, and had fallen foul of Sir Thomas Lucy, the local magnate; another that he was for some time a schoolmaster.

From 1592 onwards the records are much fuller. In March, 1592, the Lord Strange's players produced a new play at the Rose Theatre called *Harry the Sixth*, which was very successful, and was probably the *First Part of Henry VI*. In the autumn of 1592 Robert Greene, the best known of the professional writers, as he was dying wrote a letter to three fellow writers in which he warned them against the ingratitude of players in general, and in particular against an 'upstart crow' who 'supposes he is as much able to bombast out a blank verse as the best of you: and being an absolute Johannes Factotum is in his own conceit the only

7

Shake-scene in a country'. This is the first reference to Shakespeare, and the whole passage suggests that Shakespeare had become suddenly famous as a playwright. At this time Shakespeare was brought into touch with Edward Alleyne the great tragedian, and Christopher Marlowe, whose thundering parts of Tamburlaine, the Jew of Malta, and Dr Faustus Alleyne was acting, as well as Hieronimo, the hero of Kyd's *Spanish Tragedy*, the most famous of all Elizabethan plays.

In April, 1593, Shakespeare published his poem *Venus and Adonis*, which was dedicated to the young Earl of Southampton: it was a great and lasting success, and was reprinted nine times in the next few years. In May, 1594, his second poem, *The Rape of Lucrece*, was also dedicated to Southampton.

There was little playing in 1593, for the theatres were shut during a severe outbreak of the plague; but in the autumn of 1594, when the plague ceased, the playing companies were reorganized, and Shakespeare became a sharer in the Lord Chamberlain's company who went to play in the Theatre in Shoreditch. During these months Marlowe and Kyd had died. Shakespeare was thus for a time without a rival. He had already written the three parts of *Henry VI*, *Richard III*, *Titus Andronicus*, *The Two Gentlemen of Verona*, *Love's Labour's Lost*, *The Comedy of Errors*, and *The Taming of the Shrew*. Soon afterwards he wrote the first of his greater plays – *Romeo and Juliet* – and he followed this success in the next three years with *A Midsummer Night's Dream*, *Richard II*, and *The Merchant of Venice*. The two parts of *Henry IV*, introducing Falstaff, the most popular of all his comic characters, were written in 1597-8.

The company left the Theatre in 1597 owing to disputes over a renewal of the ground lease, and went to play at the

Curtain in the same neighbourhood. The disputes continued throughout 1598, and at Christmas the players settled the matter by demolishing the old Theatre and re-erecting a new playhouse on the South bank of the Thames, near Southwark Cathedral. This playhouse was named the Globe. The expenses of the new building were shared by the chief members of the Company, including Shakespeare, who was by now a man of some means. In 1596 he had bought New Place, a large house in the centre of Stratford, for £60, and through his father purchased a coat-of-arms from the Heralds, which was the official recognition that he and his family were gentlefolk.

By the summer of 1598 Shakespeare was recognized as the greatest of English dramatists. Booksellers were printing his more popular plays, at times even in pirated or stolen versions, and he received a remarkable tribute from a young writer named Francis Meres, in his book *Palladis Tamia*. In a long catalogue of English authors Meres gave Shakespeare more prominence than any other writer, and mentioned by name twelve of his plays.

Shortly before the Globe was opened, Shakespeare had completed the cycle of plays dealing with the whole story of the Wars of the Roses with *Henry V*. It was followed by *As You Like it*, and *Julius Caesar*, the first of the maturer tragedies. In the next three years he wrote *Troylus and Cressida*, *The Merry Wives of Windsor*, *Hamlet*, and *Twelfth Night*.

On March 24, 1603, Queen Elizabeth died. The company had often performed before her, but they found her successor a far more enthusiastic patron. One of the first acts of King James was to take over the company and to promote them to be his own servants so that henceforward they were known as the King's Men. They acted now very frequently at Court, and prospered accordingly. In the early years of the reign Shakespeare wrote the more sombre comedies, *All's Well that Ends Well,* and *Measure for Measure,* which were followed by *Othello, Macbeth,* and *King Lear.* Then he returned to Roman themes with *Antony and Cleopatra* and *Coriolanus.*

Since 1601 Shakespeare had been writing less, and there were now a number of rival dramatists who were introducing new styles of drama, particularly Ben Jonson (whose first successful comedy, *Every Man in his Humour,* was acted by Shakespeare's company in 1598), Chapman, Dekker, Marston, and Beaumont and Fletcher who began to write in 1607. In 1608 the King's Men acquired a second playhouse, an indoor private theatre in the fashionable quarter of the Blackfriars. At private theatres, plays were performed indoors; the prices charged were higher than in the public playhouses, and the audience consequently was more select. Shakespeare seems to have retired from the stage about this time: his name does not occur in the various lists of players after 1607. Henceforward he lived for the most part at Stratford, where he was regarded as one of the most important citizens. He still wrote a few plays, and he tried his hand at the new form of tragi-comedy – a play with tragic incidents but a happy ending – which Beaumont and Fletcher had popularized. He wrote four of these – *Pericles, Cymbeline, The Winter's Tale,* and *The Tempest,* which was acted at Court in 1611. For the last four years of his life he lived in retirement. His son Hamnet had died in 1596: his two daughters were now married. Shakespeare died at Stratford upon Avon on April 23, 1616, and was buried in the chancel of the church, before the high altar. Shortly afterwards a memorial which still exists, with a portrait bust, was set up on the North wall. His wife survived him.

When Shakespeare died fourteen of his plays had been separately published in Quarto booklets. In 1623 his surviving fellow actors, John Heming and Henry Condell, with the co-operation of a number of printers, published a collected edition of thirty-six plays in one Folio volume, with an engraved portrait, memorial verses by Ben Jonson and others, and an Epistle to the Reader in which Heming and Condell make the interesting note that Shakespeare's 'hand and mind went together, and what he thought, he uttered with that easiness that we have scarce received from him a blot in his papers.'

The plays as printed in the Quartos or the Folio differ considerably from the usual modern text. They are often not divided into scenes, and sometimes not even into acts. Nor are there place-headings at the beginning of each scene, because in the Elizabethan theatre there was no scenery. They are carelessly printed and the spelling is erratic.

THE ELIZABETHAN THEATRE

Although plays of one sort and another had been acted for many generations, no permanent playhouse was erected in England until 1576. In the 1570's the Lord Mayor and Aldermen of the City of London and the players were constantly at variance. As a result James Burbage, then the leader of the great Earl of Leicester's players, decided that he would erect a playhouse outside the jurisdiction of the Lord Mayor, where the players would no longer be hindered by the authorities. Accordingly in 1576 he built the Theatre in Shoreditch, at that time a suburb of London. The experiment was successful, and by 1592 there were two more playhouses in London, the Curtain (also in Shoreditch, and the Rose on the south bank of the river, near Southwark Cathedral.

Elizabethan players were accustomed to act on a variety of stages; in the great hall of a nobleman's house, or one of the Queen's palaces, in town halls and in yards, as well as their own theatre.

The public playhouse for which most of Shakespeare's plays were written was a small and intimate affair. The outside measurement of the Fortune Theatre, which was built in 1600 to rival the new Globe, was but eighty feet square. Playhouses were usually circular or octagonal, with three tiers of galleries looking down upon the yard or pit, which was open to the sky. The stage jutted out into the yard so that the actors came forward into the midst of their audience.

Over the stage there was a roof, and on either side doors by which the characters entered or disappeared. Over the back of the stage ran a gallery or upper stage which was used whenever an upper scene was needed, as when Romeo climbs up to Juliet's bedroom, or the citizens of Angiers address King John from the walls. The space beneath this upper stage was known as the tiring house; it was concealed from the audience by a curtain which would be drawn back to reveal an inner stage, for such scenes as the witches' cave in Macbeth, Prospero's cell or Juliet's tomb.

There was no general curtain concealing the whole stage, so that all scenes on the main stage began with an entrance and ended with an exit. Thus in tragedies the dead must be carried away. There was no scenery, and therefore no limit to the number of scenes, for a scene came to an end when the characters left the stage. When it was necessary for the exact locality of a scene to be known, then Shakespeare

THE GLOBE THEATRE

Wood–engraving by R. J. Beedham after a reconstruction by J. C. Adams

indicated it in the dialogue; otherwise a simple property
or a garment was sufficient; a chair or stool showed an indoor scene, a man wearing riding boots was a messenger, a
king wearing armour was on the battlefield, or the like.
Such simplicity was on the whole an advantage; the spec-
tator was not distracted by the setting and Shakespeare was
able to use as many scenes as he wished. The action passed
by very quickly: a play of 2500 lines of verse could be acted
in two hours. Moreover, since the actor was so close to his
audience, the slightest subtlety of voice and gesture was
easily appreciated.

The company was a 'Fellowship of Players', who were
all partners and sharers. There were usually ten to fifteen
full members, with three or four boys, and some paid servants. Shakespeare had therefore to write for his team.
The chief actor in the company was Richard Burbage, who
first distinguished himself as Richard III; for him Shakespeare wrote his great tragic parts. An important member
of the company was the clown or low comedian. From
1594 to 1600 the company's clown was Will Kemp; he was
succeeded by Robert Armin. No women were allowed to
appear on the stage, and all women's parts were taken by
boys.

THE TRAGEDY OF KING LEAR

On 26th November 1607 Nathaniel Butter and John Busby entered in the Register of the Stationers' Company, and so claimed their right to print, 'A book called Master William Shakespeare his history of King Lear, as it was played before the King's Majesty at Whitehall upon Saint Stephen's night at Christmas last, by his majesty's servants playing usually at the Globe on the Bankside.' A few weeks later the play was on sale with a full and elaborate title page, as: 'Printed for Nathaniel Butter, and are to be sold at his shop in Paul's Church-yard at the sign of the Pied Bull near St. Austin's Gate. 1608.'

Lear was thus acted at King James's Court in the Christmas holidays of 1606, and various evidences show that it was a recent play written whilst the vast apprehensions, gloom and horror caused by the discovery of the Gunpowder Plot and other alarms of the 'Black Year' were still fresh. One passage in particular is datable.

Gloucester's observations on 'these late eclipses in the sun and moon' which Edmund echoes a little later to Edgar [p. 36 l. 28 and p. 37 l. 27] have been taken to refer to notable eclipses of the moon and sun on 27th September and 2nd October 1605. Actually Shakespeare took these speeches from a little pamphlet called *Strange, fearful and true news which happened at Carlstadt in the Kingdom of Croatia*. It was translated from the High Dutch and told of terrible signs and portents, which (according to the editor, one Edward

Gresham, an almanack maker) were divine portents of threatening disaster.

'The Earth's and Moon's late and horrible obscurations, the frequent eclipsations of the fixed bodies; by the wandering, the fixed stars, I mean the planets, within these few years more than ordinary, shall without doubt (salved divine inhibition) have their effects no less admirable, than the positions unusual. Which PEUCER with many more too long to rehearse out of continual observation and the consent of all authors noted to be, new leagues, traitorous designments, catching at kingdoms, translation of empire, downfall of men in authority, emulations, ambition, innovations, factious sects, schisms and much disturbance and troubles in religion and matters of the Church, with many other things infallible in sequent such orbical positions and phenomenas.'

The preface to this work of a 'sectary astronomical' was dated 11 February 1606. The similarity of phrase, rhythm and sentiment is so close that it can hardly be accidental.

It is perhaps worth noting that on 29 March 1606 there was a tempest of exceptional violence which wrought great damage all over Europe. There is no trace of a storm in any of the other versions of the Lear story, or in the old play, and it is not perhaps too far fetched to suggest that the storm scenes in *King Lear* came to Shakespeare in that wild night.

Shakespeare took a few details from another book, to make up the vocabulary of Edgar when disguised as 'poor Tom the Bedlam beggar':

'... five fiends have been in poor Tom at once, of lust, as Obidicut, Hobbididance Prince of dumbness, Mahu of stealing, Modo of murder, Flibbertigibbet of mopping and mowing, who since possesses chambermaids and waiting women.'

These names came from *A declaration of egregious popish impostures to withdraw the hearts of her Majesty's subjects from their allegiance, and from the truth of the Christian religion, professed in England, under the pretence of casting out devils.* This book, which was published early in 1603, was written by the Rev. Samuel Harsnett, Chaplain to the Bishop of London, Harsnett had taken a considerable part in the controversies which raged round John Darrell, the Puritan exorcist in 1600 and 1601, and had written the official exposure of Darrell's claims. After the controversy had died down, Harsnett turned his attention to Jesuit exorcists and in *The Declaration* he compiled an uproarious and vulgar attack on exorcism, belief in witchcraft, and superstitious practices in general.

Other echoes of events in 1605 and 1606 to be found in the play are recorded in the notes.

The story of King Lear and his three daughters was well known. It was one of many fables which old chroniclers inserted in the dark background of the times before the recorded history of England begins. King Lear (or Leir) according to Geoffrey of Monmouth, was a contemporary of Joash, King of Israel. Geoffrey's 'history' was taken over by Holinshed, in whose *Chronicles* both Lear and Cordelia are given portraits: as the supply of wood blocks was limited the same portraits are used again a few pages later for other sovereigns.

There are various versions of the story, but all agree in the general outline, which is, that after Leir had foolishly disinherited his youngest daughter (whom Spenser called Cordelia, but the other versions Cordeil or Cordella), he was driven out, and made his way to France. Cordelia received him kindly, and raised an army to war on his enemies:

> 'So to his crown she him restor'd again,
> In which he died, made ripe for death by eld,
> And after will'd, it should to her remain:
> Who peaceably the same long time did weld:
> And all men's hearts in due obedience held:
> Till that her sisters' children, woxen strong,
> Through proud ambition, against her rebelled,
> And overcommen kept in prison long,
> Till weary of that wretched life, herself she hong.'
>
> [*The Faerie Queene*, II. x. 32.]

The story had been dramatized at least twelve years before, and was acted twice at the Rose Theatre in April 1594 by the combined company of the Queen's and Sussex's men. This play, or another, was published in 1605 as *The True Chronicle History of King Leir and his three daughters, Gonorill, Ragan and Cordella*. It is possible that this crude production led Shakespeare to consider the story as suitable to his own purposes; but he took very little from the old play, which bears as little resemblance as can be to his tragedy, except for the one incident of Lear kneeling for Cordelia's forgiveness, and even this the author of *King Leir* made unintentionally comic.

According to the play Leir, after much wandering with his faithful courtier, Perillus, at last reaches the French king and Cordella, whom he does not recognize. Leir tells his story at some length, concluding that if Cordella:

> '... show a loving daughter's part,
> It comes of God and her, not my desert.

Cor. No doubt she will, I dare be sworn she will.

Leir. How know you that, not knowing what she is?

Cor. My self a father have a great way hence
Used me as ill as ever you did her;
Yet, that his reverend age I once might see,
I'ld creep along, to meet him on my knee.

Leir. O, no men's children are unkind but mine.

Cor. Condemn not all, because of others' crime:
But look, dear father, look, behold and see
Thy loving daughter speaketh unto thee. *She kneels.*

Leir. O, stand thou up, it is my part to kneel,
And ask forgiveness for my former faults. *He kneels.*

Cor. O, if you wish I should enjoy my breath,
Dear father, rise, or I receive my death. *He riseth.*

Leir. Then I will rise, to satisfy your mind,
But kneel again, till pardon be resigned. *He kneels.*

Cor. I pardon you: the word beseems not me:
But I do say so, for to ease your knee.
You gave me life, you were the cause that I
Am what I am, who else had never been.

Leir. But you gave life to me and to my friend,
Whose days had else, had an untimely end.'

They continue this kneeling competition for another
forty lines.

In designing his tragedy Shakespeare therefore owed
little to his predecessors. He complicates the plot by the
second story of the sorrows of Gloucester. This he seems to
have founded on a brief tale in Philip Sidney's *Arcadia* of an
old Prince of Paphlagonia who was similarly served by a
bastard son.

The text of *Lear* is very difficult; according to the list of

Modern Readings given in Professor Dover Wilson's facsimile of the Folio text there are between Quarto, Folio and edited texts about five hundred differences of reading. The Quarto published by Butter in 1608 is very badly printed. Many verse lines are printed as prose; the punctuation is chaotic; and misprints and meaningless phrases are common. This Quarto was reprinted in 1619 but falsely dated 1608. The version of the play printed in the First Folio was evidently based on a copy of the Quarto text, very carefully corrected and much revised throughout. About 300 lines of the Quarto were omitted, and some new passages not in the Quarto were added. There is nothing to show whether Shakespeare or one of his company made this revision, but the Folio certainly presents the text of the play used by the Company, and is therefore to be preferred.

The 'accepted' modern text is made up of a combination of both Quarto and Folio. The present text is based on the Folio, passages omitted in the Folio being added in brackets []. The Folio text has been followed closely. Spelling is modernized, but the original arrangement, and the punctuation (which according to Elizabethan practice 'points' the texts for reading aloud) have been kept, except where they seemed obviously wrong. A few stage directions from the Quarto have been added, and some emendations generally accepted by editors have been kept. The reader who is used to the 'accepted text' may thus find certain unfamiliarities, especially as in 'the accepted text' the readings of the Quarto are often preferred to those of the Folio, but the text itself is nearer to that used in Shakespeare's own playhouse.

*

The Tragedy of
King Lear

THE ACTORS' NAMES

LEAR, King of Britain
KING OF FRANCE
DUKE OF BURGUNDY
DUKE OF CORNWALL
DUKE OF ALBANY
EARL OF KENT
EARL OF GLOUCESTER
EDGAR, son to Gloucester
EDMUND, bastard son to Gloucester
CURAN, a courtier
Old Man, tenant to Gloucester
Doctor
Fool
OSWALD, Steward to Goneril
A Captain employed by Edmund
Gentleman attendant on Cordelia
A Herald
Servants to Cornwall
GONERIL,   ⎫
REGAN,   ⎬ daughters to Lear
CORDELIA,   ⎭

*

Enter Kent, Gloucester and Bastard.

KENT: I thought the King had more affected the Duke of
Albany, than Cornwall.

GLOUCESTER: It did always seem so to us: but now in the 5
division of the Kingdom, it appears not which of the
Dukes he values most, for equalities are so weigh'd, that
curiosity in neither, can make choice of either's moiety.

KENT: Is not this your son, my Lord?

GLOUCESTER: His breeding sir, hath been at my charge. I 10
have so often blush'd to acknowledge him, that now I am
braz'd to't.

KENT: I cannot conceive you.

GLOUCESTER: Sir, this young fellow's mother could;
whereupon she grew round-womb'd, and had indeed, 15
sir, a son for her cradle, ere she had a husband for her bed.
Do you smell a fault?

KENT: I cannot wish the fault undone, the issue of it, being
so proper.

GLOUCESTER: But I have a son, sir, by order of Law, some 20
year elder than this; who, yet is no dearer in my account,
though this knave came something saucily into the world
before he was sent for: yet was his mother fair, there was
good sport at his making, and the whoreson must be ac-
knowledged. Do you know this noble gentleman, Ed- 25
mund?

BASTARD: No, my Lord.

GLOUCESTER: My Lord of Kent: remember him here-
after, as my honourable friend.

BASTARD: My services to your Lordship. 30

KENT: I must love you, and sue to know you better.

BASTARD: Sir, I shall study deserving.

GLOUCESTER: He hath been out nine years, and away he
shall again. The King is coming.

5   *Sound a Sennet. Enter one bearing a Coronet; then Lear;
then the Dukes of Albany and Cornwall; next Goneril,
Regan, and Cordelia; with followers.*

LEAR: Attend the Lords of France and Burgundy, Gloucester.

10 GLOUCESTER: I shall, my Lord.
                    Exeunt Gloucester and Edmund.

LEAR: Meantime we shall express our darker purpose.
       Give me the map there. Know, that we have divided
       In three our Kingdom: and 'tis our fast intent,
15   To shake all cares and business from our age,
       Conferring them on younger strengths, while we
       Unburthen'd crawl toward death. Our son of Cornwall,
       And you our no less loving son of Albany,
       We have this hour a constant will to publish
20   Our daughters' several dowers, that future strife
       May be prevented now. The Princes, France and Bur-
            gundy,
       Great rivals in our youngest daughter's love,
       Long in our Court, have made their amorous sojourn,
25   And here are to be answer'd. Tell me my daughters
       (Since now we will divest us both of rule,
       Interest of territory, cares of state)
       Which of you shall we say doth love us most,
       That we, our largest bounty may extend
30   Where Nature doth with merit challenge. Goneril,
       Our eldest born, speak first.

GONERIL: Sir, I love you more than word can wield the
       matter,

Dearer than eye-sight, space, and liberty,
Beyond what can be valued, rich or rare,
No less than life, with grace, health, beauty, honour:
As much as child e'er lov'd, or father found.
A love that makes breath poor, and speech unable,   5
Beyond all manner of so much I love you.

CORDELIA: What shall Cordelia speak? Love, and be
    silent.

LEAR: Of all these bounds even from this line, to this,
    With shadowy forests, and with champains rich'd   10
    With plenteous rivers, and wide-skirted meads,
    We make thee Lady. To thine and Albany's issues
    Be this perpetual. What says our second daughter?
    Our dearest Regan, wife of Cornwall?

REGAN: I am made of that self metal as my sister   15
    And prize me at her worth. In my true heart,
    I find she names my very deed of love:
    Only she comes too short, that I profess
    Myself an enemy to all other joys,
    Which the most precious square of sense possesses,   20
    And find I am alone felicitate
    In your dear Highness' love.

CORDELIA: Then poor Cordelia,
    And yet not so, since I am sure my love's
    More ponderous than my tongue.   25

LEAR: To thee, and thine hereditary ever,
    Remain this ample third of our fair Kingdom,
    No less in space, validity, and pleasure
    Than that conferr'd on Goneril. Now our Joy,
    Although our last and least; to whose young love,   30
    The vines of France, and milk of Burgundy,
    Strive to be interess'd. What can you say, to draw
    A third, more opulent than your sisters? Speak.

CORDELLA: Nothing my Lord.

LEAR: Nothing?

CORDELIA: Nothing.

LEAR: Nothing will come of nothing, speak again.

5 CORDELIA: Unhappy that I am, I cannot heave
My heart into my mouth: I love your Majesty
According to my bond, no more nor less.

LEAR: How, how Cordelia? Mend your speech a little,
Lest you may mar your Fortunes.

10 CORDELIA: Good my Lord,
You have begot me, bred me, lov'd me.
I return those duties back as are right fit,
Obey you, love you, and most honour you.
Why have my sisters husbands, if they say

15 They love you all? Happily when I shall wed,
That Lord, whose hand must take my plight, shall carry
Half my love with him, half my care, and duty,
Sure I shall never marry like my sisters
[To love my father all.]

20 LEAR: But goes thy heart with this?

CORDELIA: Ay my good Lord.

LEAR: So young, and so untender?

CORDELIA: So young my Lord, and true.

LEAR: Let it be so, thy truth then be thy dower:

25 For by the sacred radiance of the sun,
The mysteries of Hecate and the night:
By all the operation of the orbs,
From whom we do exist, and cease to be,
Here I disclaim all my paternal care,

30 Propinquity and property of blood,
And as a stranger to my heart and me,
Hold thee from this for ever. The barbarous Scythian,
Or he that makes his generation messes

To gorge his appetite, shall to my bosom
Be as well neighbour'd, pitied, and reliev'd,
As thou my sometime daughter.

KENT: Good my Liege.

LEAR: Peace Kent,   5
Come not between the Dragon and his wrath,
I lov'd her most, and thought to set my rest
On her kind nursery. Hence and avoid my sight:
So be my grave my peace, as here I give
Her father's heart from her; call France, who stirs?   10
Call Burgundy. Cornwall, and Albany,
With my two daughters' dowers, digest the third;
Let pride, which she calls plainness, marry her:
I do invest you jointly with my power,
Pre-eminence, and all the large effects   15
That troop with majesty. Ourself by monthly course,
With reservation of an hundred knights,
By you to be sustain'd, shall our abode
Make with you by due turn, only we shall retain
The name, and all th' addition to a King: 20
The sway, revenue, execution of the rest,
Beloved sons be yours, which to confirm,
This coronet part between you.

KENT: Royal Lear,
Whom I have ever honour'd as my King,   25
Lov'd as my father, as my master follow'd,
As my great patron thought on in my prayers.

LEAR: The bow is bent and drawn, make from the
    shaft.

KENT: Let it fall rather, though the fork invade   30
The region of my heart, be Kent unmannerly,
When Lear is mad, what would'st thou do old man?
Think'st thou that duty shall have dread to speak,

When power to flattery bows? To plainness honour's
   bound,
When Majesty falls to folly; reserve thy state,
And in thy best consideration check
5   This hideous rashness, answer my life, my judgement:
Thy youngest daughter does not love thee least,
Nor are those empty-hearted, whose low sounds
Reverb no hollowness.

LEAR: Kent, on thy life no more.

10 KENT: My life I never held but as a pawn
To wage against thine enemies, ne'er fear to lose it,
Thy safety being the motive.

LEAR: Out of my sight.

KENT: See better Lear, and let me still remain
15 The true blank of thine eye.

LEAR: Now by Apollo.

KENT: Now by Apollo, King,
Thou swear'st thy Gods in vain.

LEAR: O vassal! Miscreant.

20 ALBANY, CORNWALL: Dear sir forbear.

KENT: Kill thy physician, and thy fee bestow
Upon the foul disease, revoke thy gift,
Or whilst I can vent clamour from my throat,
I'll tell thee thou dost evil.

25 LEAR: Hear me recreant, on thine allegiance hear me;
Since thou hast sought to make us break our vows,
Which we durst never yet; and with strain'd pride,
To come betwixt our sentences, and our power,
Which, nor our nature, nor our place can bear;
30 Our potency made good, take thy reward.
Five days we do allot thee for provision,
To shield thee from disasters of the world,
And on the sixth to turn thy hated back

Upon our kingdom; if on the tenth day following,
Thy banish'd trunk be found in our Dominions,
The moment is thy death, away. By Jupiter,
This shall not be revok'd.

KENT: Fare thee well, King, sith thus thou wilt appear,   5
Freedom lives hence, and banishment is here;
The Gods to their dear shelter take thee maid,
That justly think'st, and hast most rightly said:
And your large speeches, may your deeds approve,
That good effects may spring from words of love: 10
Thus Kent, O Princes, bids you all adieu,
He'll shape his old course, in a country new.

Exit.

Flourish. Enter Gloucester with France and Burgundy,
Attendants.   15

GLOUCESTER: Here's France and Burgundy, my noble
Lord.

LEAR: My Lord of Burgundy,
We first address toward you, who with this King
Hath rivall'd for our daughter; what in the least   20
Will you require in present dower with her,
Or cease your quest of love?

BURGUNDY: Most Royal Majesty,
I crave no more than hath your Highness offer'd,
Nor will you tender less?   25

LEAR: Right noble Burgundy,
When she was dear to us, we did hold her so,
But now her price is fallen: sir, there she stands,
If aught within that little seeming substance,
Or all of it with our displeasure piec'd,   30
And nothing more may fitly like your Grace,
She's there, and she is yours.

BURGUNDY: I know no answer.

LEAR: Will you with those infirmities she owes,
    Unfriended, new-adopted to our hate,
    Dower'd with our curse, and stranger'd with our oath,
    Take her, or leave her?

5 BURGUNDY: Pardon me royal sir,
    Election makes not up in such conditions.

LEAR: Then leave her sir, for by the power that made me,
    I tell you all her wealth. For you great King,
    I would not from your love make such a stray,
10   To match you where I hate, therefore beseech you
    T' avert your liking a more worthier way,
    Than on a wretch whom Nature is asham'd
    Almost t' acknowledge hers.

FRANCE: This is most strange,
15   That she whom even but now, was your best object,
    The argument of your praise, balm of your age,
    The best, the dearest, should in this trice of time
    Commit a thing so monstrous, to dismantle
    So many folds of favour: sure her offence
20   Must be of such unnatural degree,
    That monsters it: or your fore-vouch'd affection
    Fall into taint, which to believe of her
    Must be a faith that reason without miracle
    Should never plant in me.

25 CORDELIA: I yet beseech your Majesty.
    If for I want that glib and oily art,
    To speak and purpose not, since what I will intend,
    I'll do 't before I speak, that you make known
    It is no vicious blot, murther, or foulness,
30   No unchaste action, or dishonour'd step
    That hath depriv'd me of your grace and favour,
    But even for want of that, for which I am richer,
    A still-soliciting eye, and such a tongue,

That I am glad I have not, though not to have it,
Hath lost me in your liking.

LEAR: Better thou
Hadst not been born, than not t' have pleas'd me better.

FRANCE: Is it but this? A tardiness in nature,   5
Which often leaves the history unspoke
That it intends to do: my Lord of Burgundy,
What say you to the Lady? Love's not love
When it is mingled with regards, that stands
Aloof from th' intire point, will you have her?   10
She is herself a dowry.

BURGUNDY: Royal King,
Give but that portion which yourself propos'd,
And here I take Cordelia by the hand,
Duchess of Burgundy.   15

LEAR: Nothing, I have sworn, I am firm.

BURGUNDY: I am sorry then you have so lost a father,
That you must lose a husband.

CORDELIA: Peace be with Burgundy,
Since that respect and Fortune are his love,   20
I shall not be his wife.

FRANCE: Fairest Cordelia, that art most rich being poor,
Most choice forsaken, and most lov'd despis'd,
Thee and thy virtues here I seize upon,
Be it lawful I take up what's cast away.   25
Gods, Gods! 'Tis strange, that from their cold'st neglect
My love should kindle to inflam'd respect.
Thy dowerless daughter King, thrown to my chance,
Is Queen of us, of ours, and our fair France:
Not all the Dukes of wat'rish Burgundy,   30
Can buy this unpriz'd precious maid of me.
Bid them farewell Cordelia, though unkind,
Thou losest here a better where to find.

LEAR: Thou hast her France, let her be thine, for we
Have no such daughter, nor shall ever see
That face of hers again, therefore be gone,
Without our grace, our love, our benison:
5 Come noble Burgundy.

Flourish. Exeunt all but France, Goneril, Regan,
and Cordelia.

FRANCE: Bid farewell to your sisters.

CORDELIA: The jewels of our father, with wash'd eyes
10 Cordelia leaves you, I know you what you are,
And like a sister am most loath to call
Your faults as they are named. Love well our father:
To your professed bosoms I commit him,
But yet alas, stood I within his grace,
15 I would prefer him to a better place,
So farewell to you both.

REGAN: Prescribe not us our duties.

GONERIL: Let your study
Be to content your Lord, who hath receiv'd you
20 At Fortune's alms; you have obedience scanted,
And well are worth the want that you have wanted.

CORDELIA: Time shall unfold what plighted cunning
hides,
Who cover faults, at last with shame derides:
25 Well may you prosper.

FRANCE: Come my fair Cordelia.

Exeunt France and Cordelia.

GONERIL: Sister, it is not a little I have to say, of what most
nearly appertains to us both; I think our father will hence
30 to-night.

REGAN: That's most certain, and with you: next month
with us.

GONERIL: You see how full of changes his age is, the

observation we have made of it hath not been little; he always lov'd our sister most, and with what poor judgement he hath now cast her off, appears too grossly.

REGAN: 'Tis the infirmity of his age, yet he hath ever but slenderly known himself.   5

GONERIL: The best and soundest of his time hath been but rash, then must we look from his age, to receive not alone the imperfections of long-ingraffed condition, but therewithal the unruly waywardness, that infirm and choleric years bring with them.   10

REGAN: Such unconstant starts are we like to have from him, as this of Kent's banishment.

GONERIL: There is further compliment of leave-taking between France and him, pray you let's sit together, if our father carry authority with such disposition as he bears,   15 this last surrender of his will but offend us.

REGAN: We shall further think of it.

GONERIL: We must do something, and i' th' heat.
                        Exeunt.

I. 2   20

Enter Bastard.

BASTARD: Thou Nature art my Goddess, to thy Law
My services are bound, wherefore should I
Stand in the plague of custom, and permit
The curiosity of Nations, to deprive me?   25
For that I am some twelve, or fourteen moonshines
Lag of a brother? Why bastard? Wherefore base?
When my dimensions are as well compact,
My mind as generous, and my shape as true
As honest madam's issue? Why brand they us   30
With base? With baseness bastardy? Base, base?

Who in the lusty stealth of Nature, take
More composition, and fierce quality,
Than doth within a dull stale tired bed
Go to th' creating a whole tribe of fops
5   Got 'tween a sleep, and wake? Well then,
Legitimate Edgar, I must have your land;
Our father's love, is to the bastard Edmund,
As to th' legitimate: fine word: legitimate.
Well, my legitimate, if this letter speed,
10   And my invention thrive, Edmund the base
Shall to th' legitimate: I grow, I prosper:
Now Gods, stand up for bastards.

Enter Gloucester.

GLOUCESTER: Kent banish'd thus and France in choler
15   parted?
And the King gone to-night? Prescrib'd his power,
Confin'd to exhibition? All this done
Upon the gad? Edmund, how now? What news?

BASTARD: So please your Lordship, none.

20 GLOUCESTER: Why so earnestly seek you to put up that
      letter?

BASTARD: I know no news, my Lord.

GLOUCESTER: What paper were you reading?

BASTARD: Nothing my Lord.

25 GLOUCESTER: No? what needed then that terrible dispatch of it into your pocket? the quality of nothing, hath
not such need to hide itself. Let's see: come, if it be nothing, I shall not need spectacles.

BASTARD: I beseech you sir, pardon me; it is a letter from
30   my brother, that I have not all o'er-read; and for so much
as I have perus'd, I find it not fit for your o'er-looking.

GLOUCESTER: Give me the letter, sir.

BASTARD: I shall offend, either to detain, or give it:

the contents, as in part I understand them, are to blame.

GLOUCESTER: Let's see, let's see.

BASTARD: I hope for my brother's justification, he wrote this but as an essay, or taste of my virtue. 5

GLOUCESTER reads: *This policy, and reverence of age, makes the world bitter to the best of our times: keeps our fortunes from us, till our oldness cannot relish them. I begin to find an idle and fond bondage, in the oppression of aged tyranny, who sways not as it hath power, but as it is suffer'd. Come to me, 10 that of this I may speak more. If our father would sleep till I wak'd him, you should enjoy half his revenue for ever, and live the beloved of your brother.* EDGAR.

Hum? Conspiracy? Sleep till I wake him, you should enjoy half his revenue: my son Edgar, had he a hand to 15 write this? A heart and brain to breed it in? When came you to this? Who brought it?

BASTARD: It was not brought me, my Lord; there's the cunning of it. I found it thrown in at the casement of my closet. 20

GLOUCESTER: You know the character to be your brother's?

BASTARD: If the matter were good my Lord, I durst swear it were his: but in respect of that, I would fain think it were not.

GLOUCESTER: It is his. 25

BASTARD: It is his hand, my Lord: but I hope his heart is not in the contents.

GLOUCESTER: Has he never before sounded you in this business?

BASTARD: Never my Lord. But I have heard him oft 30 maintain it to be fit, that sons at perfect age, and fathers declin'd, the father should be as ward to the son, and the son manage his revenue.

GLOUCESTER: O villain, villain: his very opinion in the letter. Abhorred villain, unnatural, detested, brutish villain; worse than brutish: go sirrah, seek him: I'll apprehend him. Abominable villain, where is he?

5 BASTARD: I do not well know my Lord. If it shall please you to suspend your indignation against my brother, till you can derive from him better testimony of his intent, you should run a certain course: where, if you violently proceed against him, mistaking his purpose, it would

10 make a great gap in your own honour, and shake in pieces, the heart of his obedience. I dare pawn down my life for him, that he hath writ this to feel my affection to your honour, and to no other pretence of danger.

GLOUCESTER: Think you so?

15 BASTARD: If your honour judge it meet, I will place you where you shall hear us confer of this, and by an auricular assurance have your satisfaction, and that without any further delay, than this very evening.

GLOUCESTER: He cannot be such a monster.

20 [BASTARD: Nor is not sure.

GLOUCESTER: To his father, that so tenderly and entirely loves him, Heaven and Earth!] Edmund seek him out: wind me into him, I pray you: frame the business after your own wisdom. I would unstate myself, to be in a due

25 resolution.

BASTARD: I will seek him sir, presently: convey the business as I shall find means, and acquaint you withal.

GLOUCESTER: These late eclipses in the sun and moon portend no good to us: though the wisdom of Nature can

30 reason it thus, and thus, yet Nature finds itself scourg'd by the sequent effects. Love cools, friendship falls off, brothers divide. In cities, mutinies; in countries, discord; in palaces, treason; and the bond crack'd, 'twixt son and

father. This villain of mine comes under the prediction;
there's son against father; the King falls from bias of
Nature, there's father against child. We have seen the
best of our time. Machinations, hollowness, treachery,
and all ruinous disorders follow us disquietly to our 5
graves. Find out this villain, Edmund, it shall lose thee
nothing, do it carefully: and the noble and true-hearted
Kent banish'd; his offence, honesty. 'Tis strange.

Exit.

BASTARD: This is the excellent foppery of the world, that 10
when we are sick in fortune, often the surfeits of our own
behaviour, we make guilty of our disasters, the sun, the
moon, and stars, as if we were villains on necessity, fools
by heavenly compulsion, knaves, thieves, and treachers by
spherical predominance. Drunkards, liars, and adulterers 15
by an inforc'd obedience of planetary influence; and all
that we are evil in, by a divine thrusting on. An admirable evasion of whoremaster man, to lay his goatish disposition on the charge of a star. My father compounded
with my mother under the Dragon's tail, and my nativity 20
was under *Ursa Major*, so that it follows, I am rough and
lecherous. I should have been that I am, had the maiden-
liest star in the firmament twinkled on my bastardizing.

Enter Edgar.

Pat: he comes like the catastrophe of the old comedy: 25
my cue is villanous melancholy, with a sigh like Tom o'
Bedlam. – O these eclipses do portend these divisions.
Fa, sol, la, mi.

EDGAR: How now brother Edmund, what serious contem-
plation are you in? 30

BASTARD: I am thinking brother of a prediction I read this
other day, what should follow these eclipses.

EDGAR: Do you busy yourself with that?

BASTARD: I promise you, the effects he writes of, succeed
unhappily, [as of unnaturalness between the child and the
parent, death, dearth, dissolutions of ancient amities, divisions in state, menaces and maledictions against King
5 and nobles, needless diffidences, banishment of friends,
dissipation of cohorts, nuptial breaches, and I know not
what.

EDGAR: How long have you been a sectary astronomical?

BASTARD: Come, come,] when saw you my father last?

10 EDGAR: The night gone by.

BASTARD: Spake you with him?

EDGAR: Ay, two hours together.

BASTARD: Parted you in good terms? Found you no displeasure in him, by word, nor countenance?

15 EDGAR: None at all.

BASTARD: Bethink yourself wherein you may have offended him: and at my entreaty forbear his presence,
until some little time hath qualified the heat of his
displeasure, which at this instant so rageth in him, that
20 with the mischief of your person, it would scarcely allay.

EDGAR: Some villain hath done me wrong.

BASTARD: That's my fear, I pray you have a continent forbearance till the speed of his rage goes slower: and as I
say, retire with me to my lodging, from whence I will
25 fitly bring you to hear my Lord speak: pray ye go, there's
my key: if you do stir abroad, go arm'd.

EDGAR: Arm'd, brother?

BASTARD: Brother, I advise you to the best, I am no honest
man, if there be any good meaning toward you: I have
30 told you what I have seen, and heard: but faintly. Nothing like the image, and horror of it, pray you away.

EDGAR: Shall I hear from you anon?

Exit.

BASTARD: I do serve you in this business:
A credulous father, and a brother noble,
Whose nature is so far from doing harms,
That he suspects none: on whose foolish honesty
My practices ride easy: I see the business.　　　　5
Let me, if not by birth, have lands by wit,
All with me's meet, that I can fashion fit.
Exit.

I. 3

Enter Goneril, and steward.　　　　10

GONERIL: Did my father strike my gentleman for chiding
of his fool?

STEWARD: Ay Madam.

GONERIL: By day and night, he wrongs me, every hour
He flashes into one gross crime, or other,　　　　15
That sets us all at odds: I'll not endure it;
His knights grow riotous, and himself upbraids us
On every trifle. When he returns from hunting,
I will not speak with him, say I am sick.
If you come slack of former services,　　　　20
You shall do well, the fault of it I'll answer.

STEWARD: He's coming Madam, I hear him.

GONERIL: Put on what weary negligence you please,
You and your fellows: I'ld have it come to question;
If he distaste it, let him to my sister,　　　　25
Whose mind and mine I know in that are one,
[Not to be over-ruled; idle old man
That still would manage those authorities
That he hath given away, now by my life,
Old fools are babes again, and must be us'd　　　　30

With cnecks as flatteries, when they are seen abus'd]
Remember what I tell you.

STEWARD: Well Madam.

GONERIL: And let his knights have colder looks among
you:
What grows of it no matter, advise your fellows so,
[I would breed from hence occasions, and I shall,
That I may speak], I'll write straight to my sister
To hold my course; prepare for dinner.

Exeunt.

I.4

Enter Kent.

KENT: If but as well I other accents borrow,
That can my speech defuse, my good intent
May carry through itself to that full issue
For which I raz'd my likeness. Now banish'd Kent,
If thou canst serve where thou dost stand condemn'd,
So may it come, thy master whom thou lov'st,
Shall find thee full of labours.

Horns within. Enter Lear and Attendants.

LEAR: Let me not stay a jot for dinner, go get it ready: how
now, what art thou?

KENT: A man sir.

LEAR: What dost thou profess? What wouldst thou with
us?

KENT: I do profess to be no less than I seem; to serve him
truly that will put me in trust, to love him that is honest,
to converse with him that is wise and says little, to fear
judgement, to fight when I cannot choose, and to eat no
fish.

LEAR: What art thou?

KENT: A very honest-hearted fellow, and as poor as the King.

LEAR: If thou be'st as poor for a subject, as he's for a King, thou art poor enough. What wouldst thou?

KENT: Service.   5

LEAR: Who wouldst thou serve?

KENT: You.

LEAR: Dost thou know me fellow?

KENT: No sir, but you have that in your countenance, which I would fain call master.   10

LEAR: What's that?

KENT: Authority.

LEAR: What services canst thou do?

KENT: I can keep honest counsel, ride, run, mar a curious tale in telling it, and deliver a plain message bluntly: that 15 which ordinary men are fit for, I am qualified in, and the best of me, is diligence.

LEAR: How old art thou?

KENT: Not so young sir to love a woman for singing, nor so old to dote on her for any thing. I have years on my 20 back forty eight.

LEAR: Follow me, thou shalt serve me, if I like thee no worse after dinner, I will not part from thee yet. Dinner ho, dinner; where's my knave? my fool? Go you and call my fool hither.   25

Enter Steward.

You you sirrah, where's my daughter?

STEWARD: So please you –

Exit.

LEAR: What says the fellow there? Call the clotpoll back: 30 where's my fool? Ho, I think the world's asleep, how now? Where's that mongrel?

KNIGHT: He says my Lord, your daughter is not well.

LEAR: Why came not the slave back to me when I call'd him.

KNIGHT: Sir, he answered me in the roundest manner, he would not.

5 LEAR: He would not?

KNIGHT: My Lord, I know not what the matter is, but to my judgement your Highness is not entertain'd with that ceremonious affection as you were wont, there's a great abatement of kindness appears as well in the general de-
10 pendants, as in the Duke himself also, and your daughter.

LEAR: Ha? Sayest thou so?

KNIGHT: I beseech you pardon me my Lord, if I be mistaken, for my duty cannot be silent, when I think your Highness wrong'd.

15 LEAR: Thou but rememb'rest me of mine own conception, I have perceived a most faint neglect of late, which I have rather blamed as mine own jealous curiosity, than as a very pretence and purpose of unkindness; I will look further into 't: but where's my fool? I have not seen him
20 this two days.

KNIGHT: Since my young Lady's going into France sir, the fool hath much pined away.

LEAR: No more of that, I have noted it well, go you and tell my daughter, I would speak with her. Go you call
25 hither my fool:

Enter Steward.

O you sir, you, come you hither sir, who am I sir?

STEWARD: My Lady's father.

LEAR: My Lady's father? my Lord's knave, you whoreson
30 dog, you slave, you cur.

STEWARD: I am none of these my Lord, I beseech your pardon.

LEAR: Do you bandy looks with me, you rascal?

STEWARD: I'll not be strucken my Lord.

KENT: Nor tripp'd neither, you base football player.

LEAR: I thank thee fellow. Thou serv'st me, and I'll love
thee.

KENT: Come sir, arise, away, I'll teach you differences: 5
away, away, if you will measure your lubber's length
again, tarry, but away, go to, have you wisdom, so.

Exit Steward.

LEAR: Now my friendly knave I thank thee; there's earnest
of thy service.   10

Enter Fool.

FOOL: Let me hire him too, here's my coxcomb.

LEAR: How now my pretty knave, how dost thou?

FOOL: Sirrah, you were best take my coxcomb.

LEAR: Why my boy?   15

FOOL: Why? for taking one's part that's out of favour,
nay, and thou canst not smile as the wind sits, thou'lt
catch cold shortly, there, take my coxcomb; why this
fellow has banish'd two on's daughters, and did the third
a blessing against his will, if thou follow him, thou must   20
needs wear my coxcomb. How now nuncle? Would I
had two coxcombs and two daughters.

LEAR: Why my boy?

FOOL: If I gave them all my living, I'ld keep my coxcombs
myself, there's mine, beg another of thy daughters.   25

LEAR: Take heed sirrah, the whip.

FOOL: Truth's a dog must to kennel, he must be whipp'd
out, when the Lady Brach may stand by th' fire and stink.

LEAR: A pestilent gall to me.

FOOL: Sirrah, I'll teach thee a speech.   30

LEAR: Do.

FOOL: Mark it nuncle;
Have more than thou showest,

> Speak less than thou knowest,
> Lend less than thou owest,
> Ride more than thou goest,
> Learn more than thou trowest,
> 5 Set less than thou throwest;
> Leave thy drink and thy whore,
> And keep in a door,
> And thou shalt have more,
> Than two tens to a score.

10 KENT: This is nothing fool.

FOOL: Then 'tis like the breath of an unfee'd lawyer, you gave me nothing for't, can you make no use of nothing nuncle?

LEAR: Why no, boy, nothing can be made out of nothing.

15 FOOL: Prithee tell him, so much the rent of his land comes to, he will not believe a fool.

LEAR: A bitter fool.

FOOL: Dost thou know the difference my boy, between a bitter fool, and a sweet one?

20 LEAR: No lad, teach me.

[FOOL: That Lord that counsell'd thee
> To give away thy land,
> Come place him here by me,
> Do thou for him stand;
> 25 The sweet and bitter fool
> Will presently appear,
> The one in motley here,
> The other found out there.

LEAR: Dost thou call me fool boy?

30 FOOL: All thy other titles thou hast given away, that thou wast born with.

KENT: This is not altogether fool my Lord.

FOOL: No faith, Lords and great men will not let me, if I

had a monopoly out, they would have part an't, and
Ladies too, they will not let me have all the fool to my-
self, they'll be snatching;] give me an egg nuncle, and
I'll give thee two crowns.

LEAR: What two crowns shall they be?   5

FOOL: Why, after I have cut the egg i' th' middle and eat
up the meat, the two crowns of the egg; when thou
clovest thy crown i' th' middle, and gav'st away both
parts, thou bor'st thine ass on thy back o'er the dirt, thou
hadst little wit in thy bald crown, when thou gav'st thy   10
golden one away; if I speak like myself in this, let him be
whipp'd that first finds it so.

    Fools had ne'er less grace in a year,
    For wise men are grown foppish,
    And know not how their wits to wear,   15
    Their manners are so apish.

LEAR: When were you wont to be so full of songs
sirrah?

FOOL: I have used it nuncle, e'er since thou mad'st thy
daughters thy mothers, for when thou gav'st them the   20
rod, and put'st down thine own breeches,

    Then they for sudden joy did weep,
      And I for sorrow sung,
    That such a King should play bo-peep,
      And go the fools among.   25

Prithee nuncle keep a schoolmaster that can teach thy
fool to lie, I would fain learn to lie.

LEAR: And you lie sirrah, we'll have you whipp'd.

FOOL: I marvel what kin thou and thy daughters are,
they'll have me whipp'd for speaking true: thou'lt have   30
me whipp'd for lying, and sometimes I am whipp'd for
holding my peace. I had rather be any kind o' thing than
a fool, and yet I would not be thee nuncle, thou hast

pared thy wit o' both sides, and left nothing i' th' middle;
here comes one o' the parings.

Enter Goneril.

LEAR: How now daughter? what makes that frontlet
5   on? You are too much of late i' th' frown.

FOOL: Thou wast a pretty fellow when thou hadst no need
to care for her frowning, now thou art an O without a
figure, I am better than thou art now, I am a fool, thou
art nothing. Yes forsooth I will hold my tongue, so
10   your face bids me, though you say nothing Mum,
mum,

   He that keeps nor crust, nor crum,
   Weary of all, shall want some.

That's a sheal'd peascod.

15 GONERIL: Not only sir this, your all-licens'd fool,
But other of your insolent retinue
Do hourly carp and quarrel, breaking forth
In rank, and not-to-be-endur'd riots, sir.
I had thought by making this well known unto you,
20   To have found a safe redress, but now grow fearful
By what yourself too late have spoke and done,
That you protect this course, and put it on
By your allowance, which if you should, the fault
Would not 'scape censure, nor the redresses sleep,
25   Which in the tender of a wholesome weal,
Might in their working do you that offence,
Which else were shame, that then necessity
Will call discreet proceeding.

FOOL: For you know nuncle,
30   The hedge-sparrow fed the cuckoo so long,
That it's had it head bit off by it young,
So out went the candle, and we were left darkling.

LEAR: Are you our daughter?

GONERIL: I would you would make use of your good wis-
dom
(Whereof I know you are fraught) and put away
These dispositions, which of late transport you
From what you rightly are.   5
FOOL: May not an ass know, when the cart draws the
horse? Whoop Jug I love thee.
LEAR: Does any here know me? This is not Lear:
Does Lear walk thus? Speak thus? Where are his
eyes?   10
Either his notion weakens, his discernings
Are lethargied. Ha! Waking? 'Tis not so?
Who is it that can tell me who I am?
FOOL: Lear's shadow.
[LEAR: I would learn that, for by the marks of sovereignty, 15
knowledge, and reason, I should be false persuaded I had
daughters.
FOOL: Which they, will make an obedient father.]
LEAR: Your name, fair gentlewoman?
GONERIL: This admiration sir, is much o' th' savour   20
Of other your new pranks. I do beseech you
To understand my purposes aright:
As you are old, and reverend, should be wise.
Here do you keep a hundred knights and squires,
Men so disorder'd, so debosh'd, and bold,   25
That this our Court, infected with their manners,
Shows like a riotous inn; epicurism and lust
Makes it more like a tavern, or a brothel,
Than a grac'd Palace. The shame itself doth speak
For instant remedy. Be then desir'd   30
By her, that else will take the thing she begs,
A little to disquantity your train,
And the remainders that shall still depend,

    To be such men as may besort your age,
    Which know themselves, and you.
LEAR: Darkness, and devils.
    Saddle my horses: call my train together.
5   Degenerate bastard, I'll not trouble thee;
    Yet have I left a daughter.
GONERIL: You strike my people, and your disorder'd rabble,
    Make servants of their betters.
10   *Enter Albany.*
LEAR: Woe, that too late repents:
    Is it your will, speak sir? Prepare my horses.
    Ingratitude! thou marble-hearted Fiend,
    More hideous when thou show'st thee in a child,
15   Than the sea-monster.
ALBANY: Pray sir be patient.
LEAR: Detested kite, thou liest.
    My train are men of choice, and rarest parts,
    That all particulars of duty know,
20   And in the most exact regard, support
    The worships of their name. O most small fault,
    How ugly didst thou in Cordelia show?
    Which like an engine, wrench'd my frame of Nature
    From the fix'd place: drew from my heart all love.
25   And added to the gall. O Lear, Lear, Lear!
    Beat at this gate that let thy folly in,
    And thy dear judgement out. Go, go, my people.
               Exeunt Kent and Attendants.
ALBANY: My Lord, I am guiltless, as I am ignorant
30   Of what hath moved you.
LEAR: It may be so, my Lord.
    Hear Nature, hear dear Goddess, hear:
    Suspend thy purpose, if thou didst intend

To make this creature fruitful:
Into her womb convey sterility,
Dry up in her the organs of increase,
And from her derogate body never spring
A babe to honour her. If she must teem, 5
Create her child of spleen, that it may live
And be a thwart disnatur'd torment to her.
Let it stamp wrinkles in her brow of youth,
With cadent tears fret channels in her cheeks,
Turn all her mother's pains and benefits 10
To laughter, and contempt: that she may feel,
How sharper than a serpent's tooth it is,
To have a thankless child. Away, away.

Exit.

ALBANY: Now Gods that we adore, whereof comes this? 15
GONERIL: Never afflict yourself to know more of it:
But let his disposition have that scope
As dotage gives it.

Enter Lear.

LEAR: What fifty of my followers at a clap? 20
Within a fortnight?
ALBANY: What's the matter, sir?
LEAR: I'll tell thee: life and death, I am asham'd
That thou hast power to shake my manhood thus,
That these hot tears, which break from me perforce 25
Should make thee worth them. Blasts and fogs upon
thee:
Th' untented woundings of a father's curse
Pierce every sense about thee. Old fond eyes,
Beweep this cause again, I'll pluck ye out, 30
And cast you with the waters that you lose
To temper clay. Ha? Let it be so.
I have another daughter,

Who I am sure is kind and comfortable:
When she shall hear this of thee, with her nails
She'll flay thy wolvish visage. Thou shalt find,
That I'll resume the shape which thou dost think
5   I have cast off for ever.

Exit.

GONERIL: Do you mark that?
ALBANY: I cannot be so partial Goneril,
    To the great love I bear you.
10 GONERIL: Pray you content. What Oswald hoa!
    You sir, more knave than fool, after your master.
FOOL: Nuncle Lear, nuncle Lear,
    Tarry, take the fool with thee:
    A fox, when one has caught her,
15 And such a daughter,
    Should sure to the slaughter,
    If my cap would buy a halter,
    So the fool follows after.

Exit.

20 GONERIL: This man hath had good counsel, a hundred
        knights?
    'Tis politic, and safe to let him keep
    At point a hundred knights: yes, that on every dream,
    Each buzz, each fancy, each complaint, dislike,
25 He may enguard his dotage with their powers,
    And hold our lives in mercy. Oswald, I say.
ALBANY: Well, you may fear too far.
GONERIL: Safer than trust too far;
    Let me still take away the harms I fear,
30 Not fear still to be taken. I know his heart,
    What he hath utter'd I have writ my sister:
    If she sustain him, and his hundred knights
    When I have show'd th' unfitness.

Enter Steward

How now Oswald?

What have you writ that letter to my sister?

OSWALD: Ay Madam.

GONERIL: Take you some company, and away to horse,   5
Inform her full of my particular fear,
And thereto add such reasons of your own,
As may compact it more. Get you gone,
And hasten your return. (*Exit Oswald*.) No, no, my
    Lord,   10
This milky gentleness, and course of yours
Though I condemn not, yet under pardon
You are much more at task for want of wisdom,
Than prais'd for harmful mildness.

ALBANY: How far your eyes may pierce I cannot tell;   15
Striving to better, oft we mar what's well.

GONERIL: Nay then –

ALBANY: Well, well, th' event.

Exeunt.

I. 5   20

Enter Lear, Kent, Gentleman and Fool.

LEAR: Go you before to Gloucester with these letters;
acquaint my daughter no further with any thing you
know, than comes from her demand out of the letter; if
your diligence be not speedy, I shall be there afore you. 25

KENT: I will not sleep my Lord, till I have delivered your
letter.

Exit.

FOOL: If a man's brains were in's heels, were't not in
danger of kibes?   30

LEAR: Ay boy.

FOOL: Then I prithee be merry, thy wit shall not go slip-
shod.

LEAR: Ha, ha, ha.

FOOL: Shalt see thy other daughter will use thee kindly,
5   for though she's as like this, as a crab's like an apple, yet
I can tell what I can tell.

LEAR: What canst tell boy?

FOOL: She will taste as like this, as a crab does to a crab:
thou canst tell why one's nose stands i' th' middle on's
10   face?

LEAR: No.

FOOL: Why to keep one's eyes of either side's nose, that
what a man cannot smell out, he may spy into.

LEAR: I did her wrong.

15 FOOL: Canst tell how an oyster makes his shell?

LEAR: No.

FOOL: Nor I neither; but I can tell why a snail has a house.

LEAR: Why?

FOOL: Why to put's head in, not to give it away to his
20   daughters, and leave his horns without a case.

LEAR: I will forget my nature, so kind a father? Be my
horses ready?

FOOL: Thy asses are gone about 'em; the reason why the
seven stars are no mo than seven, is a pretty reason.

25 LEAR: Because they are not eight.

FOOL: Yes indeed, thou wouldst make a good fool.

LEAR: To take't again perforce; Monster Ingratitude!

FOOL: If thou wert my fool nuncle, I'ld have thee beaten
for being old before thy time.

30 LEAR: How's that?

FOOL: Thou shouldst not have been old, till thou hadst
been wise.

LEAR: O let me not be mad, not mad sweet heaven:

Keep me in temper, I would not be mad.
How now, are the horses ready?
GENTLEMAN: Ready my Lord.
LEAR: Come boy.
FOOL: She that's a maid now, and laughs at my departure,   5
 Shall not be a maid long, unless things be cut shorter.
Exeunt.

II. 1

Enter Bastard and Curan severally.

BASTARD: Save thee Curan.   10
CURAN: And you sir, I have been with your father, and
 given him notice that the Duke of Cornwall, and Regan
 his Duchess will be here with him this night.
BASTARD: How comes that?
CURAN: Nay I know not, you have heard of the news   15
 abroad, I mean the whisper'd ones, for they are yet but
 ear-kissing arguments.
BASTARD: Not I: pray you what are they?
CURAN: Have you heard of no likely wars toward, 'twixt
 the Dukes of Cornwall, and Albany?   20
BASTARD: Not a word.
CURAN: You may do then in time, fare you well sir.
Exit.

BASTARD: The Duke be here to-night? The better best,
 This weaves itself perforce into my business,   25
 My father hath set guard to take my brother,
 And I have one thing of a queasy question
 Which I must act; briefness, and fortune work.
Enter Edgar.

Brother, a word, descend; brother I say,   30
 My father watches: O sir, fly this place,

Intelligence is given where you are hid;
You have now the good advantage of the night,
Have you not spoken 'gainst the Duke of Cornwall?
He's coming hither, now i' th' night, i' th' haste,
5   And Regan with him, have you nothing said
Upon his party 'gainst the Duke of Albany?
Advise yourself.

EDGAR: I am sure on't, not a word.

BASTARD: I hear my father coming, pardon me:
10   In cunning, I must draw my sword upon you:
Draw, seem to defend yourself, now quit you well.
Yield, come before my father, light hoa, here,
Fly brother, torches, torches, so farewell.

Exit Edgar.

15   Some blood drawn on me, would beget opinion
Of my more fierce endeavour. I have seen drunkards
Do more than this in sport; father, father,
Stop, stop, no help?

Enter Gloucester, and Servants with torches.

20 GLOUCESTER: Now Edmund, where's the villain?

BASTARD: Here stood he in the dark, his sharp sword out,
Mumbling of wicked charms, conjuring the Moon
To stand auspicious mistress.

GLOUCESTER: But where is he?

25 BASTARD: Look sir, I bleed.

GLOUCESTER: Where is the villain, Edmund?

BASTARD: Fled this way sir, when by no means he could—

GLOUCESTER: Pursue him, ho: go after. By no means, what?

30 BASTARD: Pursuade me to the murther of your Lordship,
But that I told him the revenging Gods,
'Gainst parricides did all the thunder bend,
Spoke with how manifold, and strong a bond

The child was bound to th' father; sir in fine,
Seeing how loathly opposite I stood
To his unnatural purpose, in fell motion
With his prepared sword, he charges home
My unprovided body, latch'd mine arm;   5
And when he saw my best alarum'd spirits
Bold in the quarrel's right, roused to th' encounter,
Or whether gasted by the noise I made,
Full suddenly he fled.

GLOUCESTER: Let him fly far: 10
Not in this land shall he remain uncaught,
And found, dispatch; the noble Duke my master,
My worthy arch and patron comes to-night,
By his authority I will proclaim it,
That he which finds him shall deserve our thanks,   15
Bringing the murderous coward to the stake:
He that conceals him death.

BASTARD: When I dissuaded him from his intent,
And found him pight to do it, with curst speech
I threaten'd to discover him; he replied,   20
Thou unpossessing bastard, dost thou think,
If I would stand against thee, would the reposal
Of any trust, virtue, or worth in thee
Make thy words faith'd? No, what I should deny,
(As this I would, ay, though thou didst produce   25
My very character) I'ld turn it all
To thy suggestion, plot, and damned practice:
And thou must make a dullard of the world,
If they not thought the profits of my death
Were very pregnant and potential spirits   30
To make thee seek it.

Tucket within.

GLOUCESTER: O strange and fastened villain,

Would he deny his letter, said he?
Hark, the Duke's trumpets, I know not why he comes:
All ports I'll bar, the villain shall not 'scape,
The Duke must grant me that: besides, his picture
5 I will send far and near, that all the kingdom
May have due note of him, and of my land,
Loyal and natural boy, I'll work the means
To make thee capable.

Enter Cornwall, Regan, and Attendants.

10 CORNWALL: How now my noble friend, since I came hither,
(Which I can call but now) I have heard strange news.
REGAN: If it be true, all vengeance comes too short
Which can pursue th' offender; how dost my Lord?
15 GLOUCESTER: O madam, my old heart is crack'd, its crack'd.
REGAN: What, did my father's godson seek your life?
He whom my father nam'd, your Edgar?
GLOUCESTER: O Lady, Lady, shame would have it hid.
20 REGAN: Was he not companion with the riotous knights
That tended upon my father?
GLOUCESTER: I know not Madam, 'tis too bad, too bad.
BASTARD: Yes Madam, he was of that consort.
REGAN: No marvel then, though he were ill affected,
25   'Tis they have put him on the old man's death,
To have th' expense and waste of his revenues:
I have this present evening from my sister
Been well inform'd of them, and with such cautions,
That if they come to sojourn at my house,
30   I'll not be there.
CORNWALL: Nor I, assure thee Regan.
Edmund, I hear that you have shown your father
A child-like office.

BASTARD: It was my duty sir.
GLOUCESTER: He did bewray his practice, and receiv'd
  This hurt you see, striving to apprehend him.
CORNWALL: Is he pursued?
GLOUCESTER: Ay my good Lord.   5
CORNWALL: If he be taken, he shall never more
  Be fear'd of doing harm; make your own purpose,
  How in my strength you please: for you Edmund,
  Whose virtue and obedience doth this instant
  So much commend itself, you shall be ours,   10
  Natures of such deep trust, we shall much need:
  You we first seize on.
BASTARD: I shall serve you sir truly, however else.
GLOUCESTER: For him I thank your Grace.
CORNWALL: You know not why we came to visit you?   15
REGAN: Thus out of season, threading dark-ey'd night,
  Occasions noble Gloucester of some prize,
  Wherein we must have use of your advice.
  Our father he hath writ, so hath our sister,
  Of differences, which I best thought it fit   20
  To answer from our home: the several messengers
  From hence attend dispatch: our good old friend,
  Lay comforts to your bosom, and bestow
  Your needful counsel to our businesses,
  Which craves the instant use.   25
GLOUCESTER: I serve you Madam,
  Your Graces are right welcome.
                    Exeunt. Flourish.

II. 2

Enter Kent and Steward, severally.

STEWARD: Good dawning to thee friend, art of this house?

KENT: Ay.

5 STEWARD: Where may we set our horses?

KENT: I' th' mire.

STEWARD: Prithee, if thou lov'st me, tell me.

KENT: I love thee not.

STEWARD: Why then I care not for thee.

10 KENT: If I had thee in Lipsbury pinfold, I would make thee care for me.

STEWARD: Why dost thou use me thus? I know thee not.

KENT: Fellow I know thee.

STEWARD: What dost thou know me for?

15 KENT: A knave, a rascal, an eater of broken meats, a base, proud, shallow, beggarly, three-suited hundred-pound, filthy worsted-stocking knave, a lily-livered, action-taking, whoreson glass-gazing super-serviceable finical rogue, one trunk-inheriting slave, one that wouldst be a

20 bawd in way of good service, and art nothing but the composition of a knave, beggar, coward, pandar, and the son and heir of a mongrel bitch, one whom I will beat into clamorous whining, if thou deni'st the least syllable of thy addition.

25 STEWARD: Why, what a monstrous fellow art thou, thus to rail on one, that is neither known of thee, nor knows thee?

KENT: What a brazen-fac'd varlet art thou, to deny thou knowest me? Is it two days since I tripp'd up thy heels,

30 and beat thee before the King? Draw you rogue, for though it be night, yet the moon shines, I'll make a sop

o' th' moonshine of you, you whoreson cullionly barber-
monger, draw.

STEWARD: Away, I have nothing to do with thee.

KENT: Draw you rascal, you come with letters against the
King, and take Vanity the puppet's part, against the 5
royalty of her father: draw you rogue, or I'll so carbonado your shanks, draw you rascal, come your ways.

STEWARD: Help, ho, murther, help.

KENT: Strike you slave: stand rogue, stand you neat slave,
strike. 10

STEWARD: Help hoa, murther, murther.

Enter Bastard, Cornwall, Regan, Gloucester, and Servants.

BASTARD: How now, what's the matter? Part.

KENT: With you goodman boy, if you please, come, I'll
flesh ye, come on young master. 15

GLOUCESTER: Weapons? Arms? what's the matter here?

CORNWALL: Keep peace upon your lives, he dies that
strikes again, what is the matter?

REGAN: The messengers from our sister, and the King?

CORNWALL: What is your difference, speak? 20

STEWARD: I am scarce in breath my Lord.

KENT: No marvel, you have so bestirr'd your valour, you
cowardly rascal, nature disclaims in thee: a tailor made
thee.

CORNWALL: Thou art a strange fellow, a tailor make a 25
man?

KENT: A tailor sir, a stone-cutter, or a painter, could not
have made him so ill, though they had been but two
hours o' th' trade.

CORNWALL: Speak yet, how grew your quarrel? 30

STEWARD: This ancient ruffian sir, whose life I have spar'd
at suit of his grey beard.

KENT: Thou whoreson zed, thou unnecessary letter: my

Lord, if you will give me leave, I will tread this unbolted
villain into mortar, and daub the wall of a jakes with him.
Spare my grey beard, you wagtail?

CORNWALL: Peace sirrah,

5　　You beastly knave, know you no reverence?

KENT: Yes sir, but anger hath a privilege.

CORNWALL: Why art thou angry?

KENT: That such a slave as this should wear a sword,
Who wears no honesty: such smiling rogues as these,

10　　Like rats oft bite the holy cords a-twain,
Which are too intrinse t' unloose: smooth every passion
That in the natures of their Lords rebel,
Bring oil to fire, snow to the colder moods,
Renege, affirm, and turn their halcyon beaks

15　　With every gale, and vary of their masters,
Knowing nought (like dogs) but following:
A plague upon your epileptic visage,
Smile you my speeches, as I were a fool?
Goose, if I had you upon Sarum Plain,

20　　I'ld drive ye cackling home to Camelot.

CORNWALL: What art thou mad old fellow?

GLOUCESTER: How fell you out? say that.

KENT: No contraries hold more antipathy,
Than I, and such a knave.

25　CORNWALL: Why dost thou call him knave?
What is his fault?

KENT: His countenance likes me not.

CORNWALL: No more perchance does mine, nor his, nor
hers.

30　KENT: Sir, 'tis my occupation to be plain,
I have seen better faces in my time,
Than stands on any shoulder that I see
Before me, at this instant.

CORNWALL: This is some fellow,
   Who having been prais'd for bluntness, doth affect
   A saucy roughness, and constrains the garb
   Quite from his Nature. He cannot flatter he,
   An honest mind and plain, he must speak truth,   5
   And they will take it so, if not, he's plain.
   These kind of knaves I know, which in this plainness
   Harbour more craft, and more corrupter ends,
   Than twenty silly ducking observants,
   That stretch their duties nicely.   10
KENT: Sir, in good faith, in sincere verity,
   Under th' allowance of your great aspect,
   Whose influence like the wreath of radiant fire
   On flicking Phœbus' front.
CORNWALL: What mean'st by this?   15
KENT: To go out of my dialect, which you discommend
   so much; I know sir, I am no flatterer, he that beguil'd
   you in a plain accent, was a plain knave, which for my
   part I will not be, though I should win your displeasure
   to entreat me to't.   20
CORNWALL: What was th' offence you gave him?
STEWARD: I never gave him any:
   It pleas'd the King his master very late
   To strike at me upon his misconstruction,
   When he compact, and flattering his displeasure   25
   Tripp'd me behind: being down, insulted, rail'd,
   And put upon him such a deal of man,
   That worthied him, got praises of the King,
   For him attempting, who was self-subdued,
   And in the fleshment of this dread exploit,   30
   Drew on me here again.
KENT: None of these rogues, and cowards
   But Ajax is their fool.

CORNWALL: Fetch forth the stocks!
  You stubborn ancient knave, you reverend braggart,
  We'll teach you.
KENT: Sir, I am too old to learn:
5   Call not your stocks for me, I serve the King,
  On whose employment I was sent to you.
  You shall do small respects, show too bold malice
  Against the grace, and person of my master,
  Stocking his messenger.
10 CORNWALL: Fetch forth the stocks; as I have life and honour,
  There shall he sit till noon.
REGAN: Till noon? till night my Lord, and all night too.
KENT: Why Madam, if I were your father's dog,
  You should not use me so.
15 REGAN: Sir, being his knave, I will.
                    Stocks brought out.
CORNWALL: This is a fellow of the self-same colour,
  Our sister speaks of. Come, bring away the stocks.
GLOUCESTER: Let me beseech your Grace, not to do so,
20 [His fault is much, and] the good King his master
  [Will check him for't; your purpos'd low correction
  Is such, as basest and contemnest wretches
  For pilferings and most common trespasses
  Are punish'd with;] the King must take it ill,
25 That he's so slightly valued in his messenger,
  Should have him thus restrain'd.
CORNWALL: I'll answer that.
REGAN: My sister may receive it much more worse,
  To have her gentleman abus'd, assaulted,
30 [For following her affairs; put in his legs].
                    Kent is put in the stocks.
  Come my good Lord, away.
                    Exeunt all but Gloucester and Kent.

GLOUCESTER: I am sorry for thee friend, 'tis the Duke's pleasure,
Whose disposition all the world well knows
Will not be rubb'd nor stopp'd; I'll entreat for thee.

KENT: Pray do not sir, I have watch'd and travell'd 5 hard,
Some time I shall sleep out, the rest I'll whistle:
A good man's fortune may grow out at heels:
Give you good morrow.

GLOUCESTER: The Duke's to blame in this, 'twill be ill 10 taken.

Exit.

KENT: Good King, that must approve the common saw,
Thou out of Heaven's benediction com'st
To the warm sun. 15
Approach thou beacon to this under globe,
That by thy comfortable beams I may
Peruse this letter. Nothing almost sees miracles
But misery. I know 'tis from Cordelia,
Who hath most fortunately been inform'd 20
Of my obscured course. And shall find time
From this enormous state, seeking to give
Losses their remedies. All weary and o'er-watch'd,
Take vantage heavy eyes, not to behold
This shameful lodging. Fortune good night, 25
Smile once more, turn thy wheel.

Enter Edgar.

EDGAR: I heard myself proclaim'd,
And by the happy hollow of a tree,
Escap'd the hunt. No port is free, no place 30
That guard, and most unusual vigilance
Does not attend my taking. Whiles I may 'scape
I will preserve myself: and am bethought

To take the basest, and most poorest shape
That ever penury in contempt of man,
Brought near to beast; my face I'll grime with filth,
Blanket my loins, elf all my hairs in knots,
5   And with presented nakedness out-face
The winds, and persecutions of the sky;
The country gives me proof, and precedent
Of Bedlam beggars, who with roaring voices,
Strike in their numb'd and mortified arms,
10   Pins, wooden-pricks, nails, sprigs of rosemary:
And with this horrible object, from low farms,
Poor pelting villages, sheep-cotes, and mills,
Sometime with lunatic bans, sometime with prayers
Enforce their charity: poor Turlygod, poor Tom,
15   That's something yet: Edgar I nothing am.

Exit.

Enter Lear, Fool, and Gentleman.

LEAR: 'Tis strange that they should so depart from home,
And not send back my messengers.
20 GENTLEMAN: As I learn'd,
The night before, there was no purpose in them
Of this remove.
KENT: Hail to thee noble master.
LEAR: Ha? Mak'st thou this shame thy pastime?
25 KENT: No my Lord.
FOOL: Hah, ha, he wears cruel garters. Horses are tied by
the heads, dogs and bears, by th' neck, monkeys by th'
loins, and men by th' legs: when a man's over-lusty at
legs, then he wears wooden nether-stocks.
30 LEAR: What's he, that hath so much thy place mistook
To set thee here?
KENT: It is both he and she,
Your son, and daughter.

LEAR: No.

KENT: Yes.

LEAR: No I say.

KENT: I say yea.

[LEAR: No no, they would not.　　　　　　　　　5

KENT: Yes they have.]

LEAR: By Jupiter I swear no.

KENT: By Juno, I swear ay.

LEAR: They durst not do't:

　They could not, would not do't: 'tis worse than murther,　10

　To do upon respect such violent outrage:

　Resolve me with all modest haste, which way

　Thou mightst deserve, or they impose this usage,

　Coming from us.

KENT: My Lord, when at their home　　　　　　15

　I did commend your Highness' letters to them,

　Ere I was risen from the place, that show'd

　My duty kneeling, came there a reeking post,

　Stew'd in his haste, half breathless, panting forth

　From Goneril his mistress, salutations;　　　　　20

　Deliver'd letters spite of intermission,

　Which presently they read; on those contents

　They summon'd up their meiny, straight took horse,

　Commanded me to follow, and attend

　The leisure of their answer, gave me cold looks,　　25

　And meeting here the other messenger,

　Whose welcome I perceiv'd had poison'd mine,

　Being the very fellow which of late

　Display'd so saucily against your Highness,

　Having more man than wit about me, drew;　　　30

　He rais'd the house, with loud and coward cries,

　Your son and daughter found this trespass worth

　The shame which here it suffers.

FOOL: Winter's not gone yet, if the wildgeese fly that way,
    Fathers that wear rags,
    Do make their children blind,
    But fathers that bear bags,
5   Shall see their children kind.
    Fortune that arrant whore,
    Ne'er turns the key to th' poor.
But for all this thou shalt have as many dolours for thy
daughters, as thou canst tell in a year.

10 LEAR: Oh how this mother swells up toward my heart!
Hysterica passio, down thou climbing sorrow,
Thy element's below; where is this daughter?

KENT: With the Earl sir, here within.

LEAR: Follow me not, stay here.

15   *Exit.*

GENTLEMAN: Made you no more offence,
But what you speak of?

KENT: None:
How chance the King comes with so small a number?

20 FOOL: And thou hadst been set i' th' stocks for that question, thoud'st well deserv'd it.

KENT: Why fool?

FOOL: We'll set thee to school to an ant, to teach thee
there's no labouring i' th' winter. All that follow their
25 noses are led by their eyes, but blind men, and there's not
a nose among twenty, but can smell him that's stinking;
let go thy hold, when a great wheel runs down a hill, lest
it break thy neck with following. But the great one that
goes upward, let him draw thee after: when a wise man
30 gives thee better counsel, give me mine again; I would
have none but knaves follow it, since a fool gives it.
    That sir, which serves and seeks for gain,
    And follows but for form;

Will pack, when it begins to rain,
And leave thee in the storm.
But I will tarry, the fool will stay,
And let the wise man fly:
The knave turns fool that runs away,   5
The fool no knave perdy.

Enter Lear and Gloucester.

KENT: Where learn'd you this fool?

FOOL: Not i' th' stocks fool.

LEAR: Deny to speak with me?   10
They are sick, they are weary,
They have travell'd all the night? mere fetches,
The images of revolt and flying off.
Fetch me a better answer.

GLOUCESTER: My dear Lord,   15
You know the fiery quality of the Duke,
How unremoveable and fix'd he is
In his own course.

LEAR: Vengeance, plague, death, confusion:
Fiery? what quality? Why Gloucester, Gloucester,   20
I'ld speak with the Duke of Cornwall, and his wife.

GLOUCESTER: Well my good Lord, I have inform'd them
so.

LEAR: Inform'd them? Dost thou understand me man.

GLOUCESTER: Ay my good Lord.   25

LEAR: The King would speak with Cornwall,
The dear father
Would with his daughter speak, commands, 'tends, service,
Are they inform'd of this? My breath and blood: 30
Fiery? The fiery Duke, tell the hot Duke that —
No, but not yet, may be he is not well,
Infirmity doth still neglect all office,

Whereto our health is bound, we are not ourselves,
When Nature being oppress'd, commands the mind
To suffer with the body; I'll forbear,
And am fall'n out with my more headier will,
5   To take the indispos'd and sickly fit,
For the sound man. Death on my state: wherefore
Should he sit here? This act persuades me,
That this remotion of the Duke and her
Is practice only. Give me my servant forth;
10   Go tell the Duke, and's wife, I'ld speak with them:
Now, presently: bid them come forth and hear me,
Or at their chamber-door I'll beat the drum,
Till it cry sleep to death.

GLOUCESTER: I would have all well betwixt you.

15   *Exit.*

LEAR: Oh me my heart! My rising heart! But down.

FOOL: Cry to it nuncle, as the cockney did to the eels,
when she put 'em i' th' paste alive, she knapp'd 'em o'
th' coxcombs with a stick, and cried down wantons,
20   down; 'twas her brother, that in pure kindness to his
horse buttered his hay.

     Enter Cornwall, Regan, Gloucester, and Servants.

LEAR: Good morrow to you both.

CORNWALL: Hail to your Grace.

25   *Kent here set at liberty.*

REGAN: I am glad to see your Highness.

LEAR: Regan, I think you are. I know what reason
I have to think so, if thou shouldst not be glad,
I would divorce me from thy mother's tomb,
30   Sepulchring an adultress. O are you free?
Some other time for that. Beloved Regan,
Thy sister's naught: O Regan, she hath tied
Sharp-tooth'd unkindness, like a vulture here,

I can scarce speak to thee, thou'lt not believe
With how deprav'd a quality. O Regan.

REGAN: I pray you sir, take patience, I have hope
You less know how to value her desert,
Than she to scant her duty.   5

LEAR: Say? How is that?

REGAN: I cannot think my sister in the least
Would fail her obligation. If sir perchance
She have restrained the riots of your followers,
'Tis on such ground, and to such wholesome end,   10
As clears her from all blame.

LEAR: My curses on her.

REGAN: O sir, you are old,
Nature in you stands on the very verge
Of her confine: you should be rul'd, and led   15
By some discretion, that discerns your state
Better than you yourself: therefore I pray you,
That to our sister, you do make return,
Say you have wrong'd her.

LEAR: Ask her forgiveness?   20
Do you but mark how this becomes the house?
Dear daughter, I confess that I am old;
Age is unnecessary: on my knees I beg,
That you'll vouchsafe me raiment, bed, and food.

REGAN: Good sir, no more: these are unsightly tricks;   25
Return you to my sister.

LEAR: Never Regan:
She hath abated me of half my train;
Look'd black upon me, struck me with her tongue
Most serpent-like, upon the very heart.   30
All the stor'd Vengeances of Heaven fall
On her ingrateful top: strike her young bones
You taking airs, with lameness.

CORNWALL: Fie sir, fie.

LEAR: You nimble lightnings, dart your blinding flames
    Into her scornful eyes: infect her beauty,
    You fen-suck'd fogs, drawn by the powerful sun,
5   To fall, and blister.

REGAN: O the blest Gods! so will you wish on me,
    When the rash mood is on.

LEAR: No Regan, thou shalt never have my curse:
    Thy tender-hefted Nature shall not give
10 Thee o'er to harshness: her eyes are fierce, but thine
    Do comfort, and not burn. 'Tis not in thee
    To grudge my pleasures, to cut off my train,
    To bandy hasty words, to scant my sizes,
    And in conclusion, to oppose the bolt
15 Against my coming in. Thou better know'st
    The offices of Nature, bond of childhood,
    Effects of courtesy, dues of gratitude:
    Thy half o' th' Kingdom hast thou not forgot,
    Wherein I thee endow'd.

20 REGAN: Good sir, to th' purpose.

                    Tucket within.

LEAR: Who put my man i' th' stocks?

                    Enter Steward.

CORNWALL: What trumpet's that?

25 REGAN: I know't, my sister's: this approves her letter,
    That she would soon be here.
    Is your Lady come?

LEAR: This is a slave, whose easy-borrowed pride
    Dwells in the sickly grace of her he follows.
30 Out varlet, from my sight.

CORNWALL: What means your Grace?

                    Enter Goneril.

LEAR: Who stock'd my servant? Regan, I have good hope

Thou didst not know on't. Who comes here? O Heav-
ens!
If you do love old men; if your sweet sway
Allow obedience; if yourselves are old,
Make it your cause: send down, and take my part.　　5
Art not asham'd to look upon this beard?
O Regan, will you take her by the hand?

GONERIL: Why not by th' hand sir? How have I offended?
All's not offence that indiscretion finds,
And dotage terms so.　　10

LEAR: O sides, you are too tough!
Will you yet hold? How came my man i' th' stocks?

CORNWALL: I sent him there, sir: but his own disorders
Deserv'd much less advancement.

LEAR: You? Did you?　　15

REGAN: I pray you father being weak, seem so.
If till the expiration of your month
You will return and sojourn with my sister,
Dismissing half your train, come then to me,
I am now from home, and out of that provision　　20
Which shall be needful for your entertainment.

LEAR: Return to her? and fifty men dismiss'd?
No, rather I abjure all roofs, and choose
To wage against the enmity o' th' air,
To be a comrade with the wolf, and owl,　　25
Necessity's sharp pinch. Return with her?
Why the hot-blooded France, that dowerless took
Our youngest born, I could as well be brought
To knee his throne, and squire-like pension beg,
To keep base life afoot; return with her?　　30
Persuade me rather to be slave and sumpter
To this detested groom.

GONERIL: At your choice sir.

LEAR: I prithee daughter do not make me mad,
    I will not trouble thee my child: farewell:
    We'll no more meet, no more see one another.
    But yet thou art my flesh, my blood, my daughter,
5   Or rather a disease that's in my flesh,
    Which I must needs call mine. Thou art a boil,
    A plague sore, or imbossed carbuncle
    In my corrupted blood. But I'll not chide thee,
    Let shame come when it will, I do not call it,
10   I do not bid the Thunder-bearer shoot,
    Nor tell tales of thee to high-judging Jove.
    Mend when thou canst, be better at thy leisure,
    I can be patient, I can stay with Regan,
    I and my hundred knights.
15 REGAN: Not altogether so,
    I look'd not for you yet, nor am provided
    For your fit welcome, give ear sir to my sister,
    For those that mingle reason with your passion,
    Must be content to think you old, and so,
20   But she knows what she does.
    LEAR: Is this well spoken?
    REGAN: I dare avouch it sir, what fifty followers?
    Is it not well? What should you need of more?
    Yea, or so many? Sith that both charge and danger,
25   Speak 'gainst so great a number? How in one house
    Should many people, under two commands
    Hold amity? 'Tis hard, almost impossible.
  GONERIL: Why might not you my Lord, receive attend-
    ance
30   From those that she calls servants, or from mine?
    REGAN: Why not my Lord? If then they chanc'd to slack
    ye,
    We could control them; if you will come to me,

(For now I spy a danger) I entreat you
To bring but five and twenty, to no more
Will I give place or notice.

LEAR: I gave you all.

REGAN: And in good time you gave it.   5

LEAR: Made you my guardians, my depositaries,
But kept a reservation to be follow'd
With such a number. What, must I come to you
With five and twenty? Regan said you so?

REGAN: And speak't again my Lord, no more with me.   10

LEAR: Those wicked creatures yet do look well-favour'd
When others are more wicked, not being the worst
Stands in some rank of praise, I'll go with thee,
Thy fifty yet doth double five-and-twenty,
And thou art twice her love.   15

GONERIL: Hear me my Lord;
What need you five and twenty? Ten? Or five?
To follow in a house, where twice so many
Have a command to tend you?

REGAN: What need one?   20

LEAR: O reason not the need: our basest beggars
Are in the poorest thing superfluous,
Allow not Nature, more than Nature needs:
Man's life is cheap as beast's. Thou art a Lady;
If only to go warm were gorgeous,   25
Why Nature needs not what thou gorgeous wear'st,
Which scarcely keeps thee warm, but for true need,
You Heavens, give me that patience, patience I need,
You see me here, you Gods, a poor old man,
As full of grief as age, wretched in both,   30
If it be you that stirs these daughters' hearts
Against their father, fool me not so much,
To bear it tamely: touch me with noble anger,

And let not women's weapons, water-drops,
Stain my man's cheeks. No you unnatural hags,
I will have such revenges on you both,
That all the world shall— I will do such things,
5   What they are yet, I know not, but they shall be
The terrors of the earth ! You think I'll weep,
No, I'll not weep. I have full cause of weeping.

Storm and Tempest.

But this heart shall break into a hundred thousand flaws
10   Or ere I'll weep: O fool, I shall go mad.

Exit, with his followers and Gloucester.

CORNWALL: Let us withdraw, 'twill be a storm.

REGAN: This house is little, the old man and's people,
Cannot be well bestow'd.

15 GONERIL: 'Tis his own blame hath put himself from rest,
And must needs taste his folly.

REGAN: For his particular, I'll receive him gladly,
But not one follower.

GONERIL: So am I purpos'd.
20   Where is my Lord of Gloucester ?

Enter Gloucester.

CORNWALL: Follow'd the old man forth, he is return'd.

GLOUCESTER: The King is in high rage.

CORNWALL: Whither is he going ?

25 GLOUCESTER: He calls to horse, but will I know not
whither.

CORNWALL: 'Tis best to give him way, he leads himself.

GONERIL: My Lord, entreat him by no means to stay.

GLOUCESTER: Alack the night comes on, and the high
30   winds
Do sorely ruffle, for many miles about
There's scarce a bush.

REGAN: O sir, to wilful men,

The injuries that they themselves procure,
Must be their schoolmasters: shut up your doors,
He is attended with a desperate train,
And what they may incense him to, being apt,
To have his ear abus'd, wisdom bids fear.   5
CORNWALL: Shut up your doors my Lord, 'tis a wild
    night,
My Regan counsels well: come out o' th' storm.
                                    Exeunt.

III. 1   10

Storm still. Enter Kent and a Gentleman, severally.
KENT: Who's there besides foul weather?
GENTLEMAN: One minded like the weather, most un-
    quietly.
KENT: I know you: where's the King?   15
GENTLEMAN: Contending with the fretful elements;
Bids the wind blow the earth into the sea,
Or swell the curled waters 'bove the main,
That things might change, or cease; [tears his white
    hair,   20
Which the impetuous blasts with eyeless rage
Catch in their fury, and make nothing of;
Strives in his little world of man to out-scorn
The to-and-fro-conflicting wind and rain;
This night wherein the cub-drawn bear would couch,   25
The lion, and the belly-pinched wolf
Keep their fur dry, unbonneted he runs,
And bids what will take all.]
KENT: But who is with him?
GENTLEMAN: None but the fool, who labours to out-jest   30
His heart-struck injuries.

KENT: Sir, I do know you,
      And dare upon the warrant of my note
      Commend a dear thing to you. There is division
      (Although as yet the face of it is cover'd
5   With mutual cunning) 'twixt Albany, and Cornwall:
      Who have, as who have not, that their great stars
      Thron'd and set high, servants, who seem no less,
      Which are to France the spies and speculations,
      Intelligent of our state. What hath been seen,
10   Either in snuffs, and packings of the Dukes,
      Or the hard rein which both of them have borne
      Against the old kind King; or something deeper,
      Whereof (perchance) these are but furnishings;
      [But true it is, from France there comes a power
15   Into this scatter'd Kingdom, who already
      Wise in our negligence have secret feet
      In some of our best ports, and are at point
      To show their open banner. Now to you,
      If on my credit you dare build so far,
20   To make your speed to Dover, you shall find
      Some that will thank you, making just report
      Of how unnatural and bemadding sorrow
      The King hath cause to plain.
      I am a gentleman of blood and breeding,
25   And from some knowledge and assurance, offer
      This office to you.]
GENTLEMAN: I will talk further with you.
KENT: No, do not:
      For confirmation that I am much more
30   Than my out-wall, open this purse, and take
      What it contains. If you shall see Cordelia,
      (As fear not but you shall) show her this ring,
      And she will tell you who that fellow is

That yet you do not know. Fie on this storm,
I will go seek the King.

GENTLEMAN: Give me your hand, have you no more to
say?

KENT: Few words, but to effect more than all yet;   5
That when we have found the King, in which your pain
That way, I'll this: he that first lights on him,
Holla the other.

Exeunt

III.2   10

Storm still.
Enter Lear, and Fool.

LEAR: Blow winds, and crack your cheeks; rage, blow
You cataracts, and hurricanoes spout,
Till you have drench'd our steeples, drown'd the cocks.   15
You sulphurous and thought-executing fires,
Vaunt-couriers of oak-cleaving thunderbolts,
Singe my white head. And thou all-shaking thunder,
Strike flat the thick rotundity o' th' world,
Crack Nature's moulds, all germens spill at once   20
That makes ingrateful man.

FOOL: O nuncle, Court holy-water in a dry house, is better
than this rain-water out o' door. Good nuncle, in, ask thy
daughter's blessing; here's a night pities neither wise
men, nor fools.   25

LEAR: Rumble thy bellyful: spit fire, spout rain:
Nor rain, wind, thunder, fire are my daughters;
I tax not you, you elements with unkindness.
I never gave you Kingdom, call'd you children;
You owe me no subscription. Then let fall   30
Your horrible pleasure. Here I stand your slave,

A poor, infirm, weak, and despis'd old man:
But yet I call you servile ministers,
That will with two pernicious daughters join
Your high-engender'd battles, 'gainst a head
So old, and white as this. O, ho! 'tis foul.

FOOL: He that has a house to put's head in, has a good
head-piece:

> The cod-piece that will house,
> Before the head has any;
> The head, and he shall louse:
> So beggars marry many.
> The man that makes his toe,
> What he his heart should make,
> Shall of a corn cry woe,
> And turn his sleep to wake.

For there was never yet fair woman, but she made
mouths in a glass.

Enter Kent.

LEAR: No, I will be the pattern of all patience,
I will say nothing.

KENT: Who's there?

FOOL: Marry here's Grace, and a cod-piece, that's a wise
man, and a fool.

KENT: Alas sir are you here? Things that love night,
Love not such nights as these: the wrathful skies
Gallow the very wanderers of the dark
And make them keep their caves: since I was man,
Such sheets of fire, such bursts of horrid thunder,
Such groans of roaring wind, and rain, I never
Remember to have heard. Man's Nature cannot carry
Th' affliction, nor the fear.

LEAR: Let the great Gods
That keep this dreadful pudder o'er our heads,

Find out their enemies now. Tremble thou wretch,
That hast within thee undivulged crimes
Unwhipp'd of Justice. Hide thee, thou bloody hand;
Thou perjur'd, and thou simular of virtue
That art incestuous. Caitiff, to pieces shake   5
That under covert, and convenient seeming
Hast practis'd on man's life. Close pent-up guilts,
Rive your concealing continents, and cry
These dreadful summoners grace. I am a man,
More sinn'd against, than sinning.   10

KENT: Alack, bare-headed?
Gracious my Lord, hard by here is a hovel,
Some friendship will it lend you 'gainst the tempest:
Repose you there, while I to this hard house,
(More harder than the stones whereof 'tis rais'd,   15
Which even but now, demanding after you,
Deni'd me to come in) return, and force
Their scanted courtesy.

LEAR: My wits begin to turn.
Come on my boy. How dost my boy? Art cold?   20
I am cold myself. Where is this straw, my fellow?
The art of our necessities is strange,
And can make vile things precious. Come, your hovel
Poor fool, and knave, I have one part in my heart
That's sorry yet for thee.   25

FOOL: He that has and a little tiny wit,
  With heigh-ho, the wind and the rain,
Must make content with his fortunes fit,
  Though the rain it raineth every day.

LEAR: True boy: come, bring us to this hovel.   30
        Exeunt Lear and Kent.

FOOL: This is a brave night to cool a courtezan:
  I'll speak a prophecy ere I go:

When priests are more in word, than matter;
When brewers mar their malt with water;
When nobles are their tailors' tutors,
No heretics burn'd, but wenches' suitors;
5   When every case in Law, is right;
No squire in debt, nor no poor knight;
When slanders do not live in tongues;
Nor cutpurses come not to throngs;
When usurers tell their gold i' th' field,
10   And bawds, and whores, do churches build,
Then shall the Realm of Albion,
Come to great confusion:
Then comes the time, who lives to see't,
That going shall be us'd with feet.
15   This prophecy Merlin shall make, for I live before his time.

Exit.

III. 3

Enter Gloucester, and Bastard.

GLOUCESTER: Alack, alack Edmund, I like not this un-
20   natural dealing; when I desired their leave that I might
pity him, they took from me the use of mine own house,
charg'd me on pain of perpetual displeasure, neither to
speak of him, entreat for him, or any way sustain him.

BASTARD: Most savage and unnatural.

25 GLOUCESTER: Go to; say you nothing. There is division
betwixt the Dukes, and a worse matter than that: I have
received a letter this night, 'tis dangerous to be spoken, I
have lock'd the letter in my closet, these injuries the King
now bears, will be revenged home; there is part of a
30   power already footed, we must incline to the King, I will
look him, and privily relieve him; go you and maintain

talk with the Duke, that my charity be not of him perceived; if he ask for me, I am ill, and gone to bed; if I die
for it (as no less is threatened me), the King my old
master must be relieved. There is strange things toward
Edmund, pray you be careful.   5

Exit.

BASTARD: This courtesy forbid thee, shall the Duke
Instantly know, and of that letter too;
This seems a fair deserving, and must draw me
That which my father loses: no less than all;   10
The younger rises, when the old doth fall.

Exit.

III. 4

Enter Lear, Kent, and Fool.

KENT: Here is the place my Lord, good my Lord enter,   15
The tyranny of the open night's too rough
For Nature to endure.

Storm still.

LEAR: Let me alone.
KENT: Good my Lord enter here.   20
LEAR: Wilt break my heart?
KENT: I had rather break mine own, good my Lord enter.
LEAR: Thou think'st 'tis much that this contentious storm
Invades us to the skin: so 'tis to thee,
But where the greater malady is fix'd,   25
The lesser is scarce felt. Thou 'ldst shun a bear,
But if thy flight lay toward the roaring sea,
Thou 'ldst meet the bear i' th' mouth; when the mind's
free,
The body's delicate: the tempest in my mind,   30
Doth from my senses take all feeling else,

Save what beats there, filial ingratitude,
Is it not as this mouth should tear this hand
For lifting food to't? But I will punish home;
No, I will weep no more; in such a night,
5   To shut me out? Pour on, I will endure:
In such a night as this? O Regan, Goneril,
Your old kind father, whose frank heart gave all,
O that way madness lies, let me shun that:
No more of that.

10 KENT: Good my Lord enter here.

LEAR: Prithee go in thyself, seek thine own ease,
This tempest will not give me leave to ponder
On things would hurt me more; but I'll go in,
In boy, go first. You houseless poverty;

15   *Exit Fool.*

Nay get thee in; I'll pray and then I'll sleep.
Poor naked wretches, whereso'er you are
That bide the pelting of this pitiless storm,
How shall your houseless heads, and unfed sides,
20   Your loop'd, and window'd raggedness defend you
From such seasons as these? O I have ta'en
Too little care of this: take physic, Pomp,
Expose thyself to feel what wretches feel,
That thou mayst shake the superflux to them,
25   And show the Heavens more just.

                    Enter Edgar and Fool.

EDGAR: Fathom, and half, fathom and half: poor Tom.

FOOL: Come not in here nuncle, here's a spirit, help me,
help me.

30 KENT: Give me thy hand, who's there?

FOOL: A spirit, a spirit, he says his name's poor Tom.

KENT: What art thou that dost grumble there i' the straw?
Come forth.

EDGAR: Away, the foul fiend follows me, through the
sharp hawthorn blow the winds. Hum, go to thy bed,
and warm thee.

LEAR: Didst thou give all to thy daughters? And art thou
come to this?   5

EDGAR: Who gives any thing to poor Tom? Whom the
foul Fiend hath led through fire, and through flame,
through sword, and whirlpool, o'er bog, and quagmire,
that hath laid knives under his pillow, and halters in his
pew, set ratsbane by his porridge, made him proud of   10
heart, to ride on a bay trotting horse, over four-inched
bridges, to course his own shadow for a traitor. Bless thy
five wits, Tom's a-cold. O do, de, do, de, do de, bless
thee from whirlwinds, star-blasting, and taking, do poor
Tom some charity, whom the foul Fiend vexes. There   15
could I have him now, and there, and there again, and
there.

Storm still.

LEAR: Has his daughters brought him to this pass?
Couldst thou save nothing? Wouldst thou give 'em all?   20

FOOL: Nay, he reserv'd a blanket, else we had been all
sham'd.

LEAR: Now all the plagues that in the pendulous air
Hang fated o'er men's faults, light on thy daughters.

KENT: He hath no daughters sir.   25

LEAR: Death traitor, nothing could have subdued Nature
To such a lowness, but his unkind daughters.
Is it the fashion, that discarded fathers,
Should have thus little mercy on their flesh:
Judicious punishment, 'twas this flesh begot   30
Those pelican daughters.

EDGAR: Pillicock sat on Pillicock-hill,
Alow, alow, loo, loo.

FOOL: This cold night will turn us all to fools, and madmen.

EDGAR: Take heed o' the foul Fiend, obey thy parents,
keep thy words Justice, swear not, commit not with
5   man's sworn spouse; set not thy sweet heart on proud
array. Tom's a-cold.

LEAR: What hast thou been?

EDGAR: A serving-man! Proud in heart, and mind; that
curl'd my hair, wore gloves in my cap; serv'd the lust of
10   my mistress' heart, and did the act of darkness with her.
Swore as many oaths, as I spake words, and broke them
in the sweet face of Heaven. One, that slept in the con-
triving of lust, and wak'd to do it. Wine lov'd I dearly,
dice dearly; and in woman, out-paramour'd the Turk.
15   False of heart, light of ear, bloody of hand; hog in sloth,
fox in stealth, wolf in greediness, dog in madness, lion in
prey. Let not the creaking of shoes, nor the rustling of
silks, betray thy poor heart to woman. Keep thy foot out
of brothels, thy hand out of plackets, thy pen from lend-
20   ers' books, and defy the foul Fiend. Still through the
hawthorn blows the cold wind: says suum, mun, nonny,
Dolphin my boy, Boy Sesey: let him trot by.
Storm still.

LEAR: Thou wert better in a grave, than to answer with
25   thy uncover'd body, this extremity of the skies. Is man
no more than this? Consider him well. Thou ow'st the
worm no silk; the beast, no hide; the sheep, no wool;
the cat, no perfume. Ha? here's three on's are sophisticated. Thou art the thing itself; unaccommodated man, is
30   no more but such a poor, bare, forked animal as thou art.
Off, off you lendings: come, unbutton here.
Enter Gloucester with a torch.

FOOL: Prithee nuncle be contented, 'tis a naughty night to

swim in. Now a little fire in a wild field, were like an old
lecher's heart, a small spark, all the rest on's body, cold:
look, here comes a walking fire.

EDGAR: This is the foul fiend Flibbertigibbet; he begins at
curfew, and walks at first cock: he gives the web and the   5
pin, squints the eye, and makes the hare-lip; mildews the
white wheat, and hurts the poor creature of earth.

    Swithold footed thrice the old,
    He met the Night-mare, and her nine-fold;
    Bid her alight, and her troth plight,   10
    And, aroint thee witch, aroint thee.

KENT: How fares your Grace?

LEAR: What's he?

KENT: Who's there? What is't you seek?

GLOUCESTER: What are you there? Your names?   15

EDGAR: Poor Tom, that eats the swimming frog, the toad,
the todpole, the wall-newt, and the water: that in the
fury of his heart, when the foul Fiend rages, eats cow-
dung for sallets; swallows the old rat, and the ditch-dog;
drinks the green mantle of the standing pool: who is   20
whipp'd from tithing to tithing, and stock'd, punish'd,
and imprison'd: who hath had three suits to his back, six
shirts to his body:

    Horse to ride, and weapon to wear:
    But mice, and rats, and such small deer,   25
    Have been Tom's food, for seven long year:

Beware my follower. Peace Smulkin, peace thou Fiend.

GLOUCESTER: What, hath your Grace no better company?

EDGAR: The Prince of Darkness is a gentleman. Modo he's   30
call'd, and Mahu.

GLOUCESTER: Our flesh and blood, my Lord, is grown so
vile, that it doth hate what gets it.

EDGAR: Poor Tom's a-cold.

GLOUCESTER: Go in with me; my duty cannot suffer
   T' obey in all your daughters' hard commands:
   Though their injunction be to bar my doors,
5 And let this tyrannous night take hold upon you,
   Yet have I ventured to come seek you out,
   And bring you where both fire, and food is ready.

LEAR: First let me talk with this philosopher,
   What is the cause of thunder?

10 KENT: Good my Lord take his offer, go into th' house.

LEAR: I'll talk a word with this same learned Theban:
   What is your study?

EDGAR: How to prevent the Fiend, and to kill vermin.

LEAR: Let me ask you one word in private.

15 KENT: Importune him once more to go my Lord,
   His wits begin t' unsettle.

GLOUCESTER: Canst thou blame him?

Storm still.

   His daughters seek his death: ah, that good Kent,
20 He said it would be thus: poor banish'd man:
   Thou say'st the King grows mad, I'll tell thee friend
   I am almost mad myself. I had a son,
   Now outlaw'd from my blood: he sought my life
   But lately: very late: I lov'd him, friend,
25 No father his son dearer: truth to tell thee,
   The grief hath craz'd my wits. What a night's this?
   I do beseech your Grace.

LEAR: O cry you mercy, sir:
   Noble philosopher, your company.

30 EDGAR: Tom's a-cold.

GLOUCESTER: In fellow there, into th' hovel; keep thee
   warm.

LEAR: Come, let's in all.

KENT: This way, my Lord.

LEAR: With him; I will keep still with my philosopher.

KENT: Good my Lord, soothe him: let him take the fellow.

GLOUCESTER: Take him you on. 5

KENT: Sirrah, come on: go along with us.

LEAR: Come, good Athenian.

GLOUCESTER: No words, no words, hush.

EDGAR: Child Rowland to the dark Tower came,
His word was still, fie, foh, and fum, 10
I smell the blood of a British man.

Exeunt.

III. 5

Enter Cornwall, and Bastard.

CORNWALL: I will have my revenge, ere I depart his 15
house.

BASTARD: How my Lord, I may be censured, that Nature
thus gives way to Loyalty, something fears me to think
of.

CORNWALL: I now perceive, it was not altogether your 20
brother's evil disposition made him seek his death: but a
provoking merit set a-work by a reproveable badness in
himself.

BASTARD: How malicious is my fortune, that I must repent to be just? This is the letter which he spoke of; 25
which approves him an intelligent party to the advantages
of France. O Heavens! that this treason were not; or not
I the detector.

CORNWALL: Go with me to the Duchess.

BASTARD: If the matter of this paper be certain, you have 30
mighty business in hand.

CORNWALL: True or false, it hath made thee Earl of
    Gloucester: seek out where thy father is, that he may be
    ready for our apprehension.

BASTARD: If I find him comforting the King, it will stuff
5   his suspicion more fully. I will persevere in my course of
    loyalty, though the conflict be sore between that, and my
    blood.

CORNWALL: I will lay my trust upon thee; and thou shalt
    find a dear father in my love.

10   *Exeunt.*

III. 6

Enter Kent and Gloucester.

GLOUCESTER: Here is better than the open air, take it
    thankfully: I will piece out the comfort with what addi-
15   tion I can: I will not be long from you.

Exit.

KENT: All the power of his wits, have given way to his im-
    patience: the Gods reward your kindness.

Enter Lear, Edgar and Fool.

20 EDGAR: Frateretto calls me, and tells me Nero is an angler
    in the Lake of Darkness: pray innocent, and beware the
    foul Fiend.

FOOL: Prithee nuncle tell me, whether a madman be a
    gentleman, or a yeoman.

25 LEAR: A King, a King.

FOOL: No, he's a yeoman, that has a gentleman to his son:
    for he's a mad yeoman that sees his son a gentleman be-
    fore him.

LEAR: To have a thousand with red burning spits
30   Come hizzing in upon 'em.

[EDGAR: The foul fiend bites my back.

FOOL: He's mad, that trusts in the tameness of a wolf, a horse's health, a boy's love, or a whore's oath.

LEAR: It shall be done, I will arraign them straight;
Come sit thou here most learned Justice,
Thou sapient sir sit here, no you she foxes –   5

EDGAR: Look where he stands and glares, want'st thou eyes, at trial madam?
Come o'er the bourn Bessy to me.

FOOL: Her boat hath a leak,
And she must not speak,   10
Why she dares not come, over to thee.

EDGAR: The foul Friend haunts poor Tom in the voice of a nightingale, Hopdance cries in Tom's belly for two white herring, croak not black angel, I have no food for thee.   15

KENT: How do you sir ? Stand you not so amaz'd,
Will you lie down and rest upon the cushions ?

LEAR: I'll see their trial first. Bring in their evidence.
Thou robed man of justice take thy place,
And thou his yoke-fellow of equity,   20
Bench by his side; you are o' th' commission,
Sit you too.

EDGAR: Let us deal justly.
Sleepest or wakest thou jolly shepherd,
Thy sheep be in the corn,   25
And for one blast of thy minikin mouth,
Thy sheep shall take no harm.
Pur the cat is gray.

LEAR: Arraign her first, 'tis Goneril. I here take my oath before this honourable assembly, she kicked the poor   30
King her father.

FOOL: Come hither mistress, is your name Goneril ?

LEAR: She cannot deny it.

FOOL: Cry you mercy, I took you for a joint-stool.

LEAR: And here's another, whose warp'd looks proclaim
What store her heart is made on; stop her there,
Arms, arms, sword, fire, corruption in the place,
5   False justicer why hast thou let her 'scape?]

EDGAR: Bless thy five wits.

KENT: O pity: sir, where is the patience now
That you so oft have boasted to retain?

EDGAR: My tears begin to take his part so much,
10 They mar my counterfeiting.

LEAR: The little dogs, and all;
Tray, Blanch, and Sweet-heart: see, they bark at me.

EDGAR: Tom, will throw his head at them:
Avaunt you curs,
15   Be thy mouth or black or white:
Tooth that poisons if it bite:
Mastiff, greyhound, mongrel, grim,
Hound or spaniel, brach or lym:
Or bobtail tike, or trundle-tail,
20   Tom will make him weep and wail,
For with throwing thus my head,
Dogs leap the hatch, and all are fled.
Do, de, de, de: sesse: come, march to wakes and fairs,
and market-towns: poor Tom thy horn is dry.

25 LEAR: Then let them anatomize Regan: see what breeds
about her heart. Is there any cause in Nature that makes
these hard-hearts? You sir, I entertain for one of my hundred; only, I do not like the fashion of your garments.
You will say they are Persian; but let them be chang'd.

30   *Enter Gloucester*

KENT: Now good my Lord, lie here, and rest awhile.

LEAR: Make no noise, make no noise, draw the curtains:
so, so, we'll go to supper i' th' morning.

FOOL: And I'll go to bed at noon.

GLOUCESTER: Come hither friend: where is the King my
    master?

KENT: Here sir, but trouble him not, his wits are gone.

GLOUCESTER: Good friend, I prithee take him in thy   5
    arms;
  I have o'erheard a plot of death upon him:
  There is a litter ready, lay him in't,
  And drive toward Dover friend, where thou shalt meet
  Both welcome, and protection. Take up thy master,   10
  If thou shouldst dally half an hour, his life
  With thine, and all that offer to defend him,
  Stand in assured loss. Take up, take up,
  And follow me, that will to some provision
  Give thee quick conduct.   15

[KENT: Oppressed nature sleeps:
  This rest might yet have balm'd thy broken sinews,
  Which if convenience will not allow,
  Stand in hard cure. Come, help to bear thy master,
  Thou must not stay behind.]   20

GLOUCESTER: Come, come away.

Exeunt all but Edgar

[EDGAR: When we our betters see bearing our woes,
  We scarcely think our miseries our foes.
  Who alone suffers, suffers most i' th' mind,   25
  Leaving free things and happy shows behind,
  But then the mind much sufferance doth o'erskip,
  When grief hath mates, and bearing fellowship:
  How light and portable my pain seems now,
  When that which makes me bend, makes the King bow.   30
  He childed as I father'd, Tom away.
  Mark the high noises; and thyself bewray,
  When false opinion, whose wrong thoughts defile thee,

In thy just proof, repeals and reconciles thee:
What will hap more to-night, safe 'scape the King,
Lurk, lurk.

Exit.]

III. 7

Enter Cornwall, Regan, Goneril, Bastard, and Servants.

CORNWALL: Post speedily to my Lord your husband, show him this letter, the army of France is landed: seek out the traitor Gloucester.

Exit a Servant

REGAN: Hang him instantly.

GONERIL: Pluck out his eyes.

CORNWALL: Leave him to my displeasure. Edmund, keep you our sister company: the revenges we are bound to take upon your traitorous father, are not fit for your beholding. Advise the Duke where you are going, to a most festinate preparation: we are bound to the like. Our posts shall be swift, and intelligent betwixt us. Farewell dear sister, farewell my Lord of Gloucester.

Enter Steward

How now? Where's the King?

STEWARD: My Lord of Gloucester hath convey'd him hence:

Some five or six and thirty of his knights
Hot questrists after him, met him at gate,
Who, with some other of the Lords, dependants,
Are gone with him toward Dover: where they boast to have well-armed friends.

CORNWALL: Get horses for your mistress.

GONERIL: Farewell sweet Lord, and sister.

Exeunt Goneril, Bastard and Steward.

CORNWALL: Edmund farewell: go seek the traitor Glou-
   cester,
   Pinion him like a thief, bring him before us:
   Though well we may not pass upon his life
   Without the form of justice, yet our power   5
   Shall do a courtesy to our wrath, which men
   May blame, but not control.

                    Enter Gloucester and Servants.

   Who's there? The traitor?

REGAN: Ingrateful fox, 'tis he.   10

CORNWALL: Bind fast his corky arms.

GLOUCESTER: What means your Graces? Good my
   friends consider
   Your are my guests: do me no foul play, friends.

CORNWALL: Bind him I say.   15

REGAN: Hard, hard: O filthy traitor.

GLOUCESTER: Unmerciful Lady as you are, I'm none.

CORNWALL: To this chair bind him, villain, thou shalt find –

GLOUCESTER: By the kind Gods, 'tis most ignobly done
   To pluck me by the beard.   20

REGAN: So white, and such a traitor?

GLOUCESTER: Naughty Lady,
   These hairs which thou dost ravish from my chin
   Will quicken and accuse thee. I am your host,
   With robbers' hands, my hospitable favours   25
   You should not ruffle thus. What will you do?

CORNWALL: Come sir,
   What letters had you late from France?

REGAN: Be simple answer'd, for we know the truth.

CORNWALL: And what confederacy have you with the   30
   traitors, late footed in the Kingdom?

REGAN: To whose hands you have sent the lunatic King:
   Speak.

GLOUCESTER: I have a letter guessingly set down
Which came from one that's of a neutral heart,
And not from one oppos'd.

CORNWALL: Cunning.

5 REGAN: And false.

CORNWALL: Where hast thou sent the King?

GLOUCESTER: To Dover.

REGAN: Wherefore to Dover? Wast thou not charg'd at
peril?

10 CORNWALL: Wherefore to Dover? Let him answer that.

GLOUCESTER: I am tied to th' stake, and I must stand the
course.

REGAN: Wherefore to Dover?

GLOUCESTER: Because I would not see thy cruel nails

15 Pluck out his poor old eyes: nor thy fierce sister,
In his anointed flesh, stick boarish fangs.
The sea, with such a storm as his bare head,
In hell-black night indur'd, would have buoy'd up
And quench'd the stelled fires:

20 Yet poor old heart, he holp the Heavens to rain.
If wolves had at thy gate howl'd that stern time,
Thou shouldst have said, good porter turn the key:
All cruels else subscribe: but I shall see
The winged Vengeance overtake such children.

25 CORNWALL: See't shalt thou never. Fellows hold the
chair.
Upon these eyes of thine, I'll set my foot.

GLOUCESTER: He that will think to live, till he be old,
Give me some help.— O cruel! O you Gods.

30 REGAN: One side will mock another: th' other too.

CORNWALL: If you see vengeance.

FIRST SERVANT: Hold your hand, my Lord:
I have serv'd you ever since I was a child:

But better service have I never done you,
Than now to bid you hold.

REGAN: How now, you dog?

FIRST SERVANT: If you did wear a beard upon your chin,
I'd shake it on this quarrel. What do you mean?   5

CORNWALL: My villain?

They draw and fight.

FIRST SERVANT: Nay then come on, and take the chance
of anger.

REGAN: Give me thy sword. A peasant stand up thus?   10

She takes a sword, and runs at him behind.

FIRST SERVANT: Oh I am slain: my Lord, you have one
eye left
To see some mischief on him. Oh.

Dies.   15

CORNWALL: Lest it see more, prevent it; out vile jelly:
Where is thy lustre now?

GLOUCESTER: All dark and comfortless?
Where's my son Edmund?
Edmund, enkindle all the sparks of Nature   20
To quit this horrid act.

REGAN: Out treacherous villain,
Thou call'st on him, that hates thee. It was he
That made the overture of thy treasons to us:
Who is too good to pity thee.   25

GLOUCESTER: O my follies! then Edgar was abus'd;
Kind Gods, forgive me that, and prosper him.

REGAN: Go thrust him out at gates, and let him smell
His way to Dover.

Exit one with Gloucester.   30

How is't my Lord? How look you?

CORNWALL: I have receiv'd a hurt: follow me Lady;
Turn out that eyeless villain: throw this slave

Upon the dunghill: Regan, I bleed apace,
Untimely comes this hurt. Give me your arm.
                    Exeunt.
[SECOND SERVANT: I'll never care what wickedness I do,
 5   If this man come to good.
THIRD SERVANT: If she live long.
      And in the end meet the old course of death,
      Women will all turn monsters.
SECOND SERVANT: Let's follow the old Earl, and get the
10   Bedlam
      To lead him where he would: his roguish madness
      Allows itself to any thing.
THIRD SERVANT: Go thou: I'll fetch some flax and whites
      of eggs
15   To apply to his bleeding face. Now heaven help him.
                    Exeunt.]

IV. 1

Enter Edgar.
EDGAR: Yet better thus, and known to be contemn'd,
20   Than still contemn'd and flatter'd, to be worst:
      The lowest and most dejected thing of Fortune,
      Stands still in esperance, lives not in fear:
      The lamentable change is from the best,
      The worst returns to laughter. Welcome then,
25   Thou unsubstantial air that I embrace:
      The wretch that thou hast blown unto the worst,
      Owes nothing to thy blasts.
                Enter Gloucester, and an Old Man.
      But who comes here? My father poorly led?
30   World, world, O world!

But that thy strange mutations make us hate thee,
Life would not yield to age.

OLD MAN: O my good Lord, I have been your tenant, and
    your father's tenant, these fourscore years.

GLOUCESTER: Away, get thee away: good friend be gone,   5
    Thy comforts can do me no good at all,
    Thee, they may hurt.

OLD MAN: You cannot see your way.

GLOUCESTER: I have no way, and therefore want no eyes:
    I stumbled when I saw. Full oft 'tis seen,   10
    Our means secure us, and our mere defects
    Prove our commodities. O dear son Edgar,
    The food of thy abused father's wrath:
    Might I but live to see thee in my touch,
    I'ld say I had eyes again.   15

OLD MAN: How now? who's there?

EDGAR: O Gods! Who is't can say I am at the worst?
    I am worse than e'er I was.

OLD MAN: 'Tis poor mad Tom.

EDGAR: And worse I may be yet: the worst is not,   20
    So long as we can say this is the worst.

OLD MAN: Fellow, where goest?

GLOUCESTER: Is it a beggar-man?

OLD MAN: Madman, and beggar too.

GLOUCESTER: He has some reason, else he could not beg.   25
    I' th' last night's storm, I such a fellow saw;
    Which made me think a man, a worm. My son
    Came then into my mind, and yet my mind
    Was then scarce friends with him.
    I have heard more since: 30
    As flies to wanton boys, are we to th' Gods,
    They kill us for their sport.

EDGAR: How should this be?

Bad is the trade that must play fool to sorrow,
Angering itself, and others. Bless thee master.

GLOUCESTER: Is that the naked fellow?

OLD MAN: Ay, my Lord.

5 GLOUCESTER: Get thee away: if for my sake
Thou wilt o'ertake us hence a mile or twain
I' th' way toward Dover, do it for ancient love,
And bring some covering for this naked soul,
Which I'll entreat to lead me.

10 OLD MAN: Alack sir, he is mad.

GLOUCESTER: 'Tis the times' plague, when madmen lead
the blind:
Do as I bid thee, or rather do thy pleasure:
Above the rest, be gone.

15 OLD MAN: I'll bring him the best 'parel that I have,
Come on't, what will.

Exit.

GLOUCESTER: Sirrah, naked fellow.

EDGAR: Poor Tom's a-cold. I cannot daub it further.

20 GLOUCESTER: Come hither fellow.

EDGAR: And yet I must:
Bless thy sweet eyes, they bleed.

GLOUCESTER: Know'st thou the way to Dover?

EDGAR: Both stile, and gate; horse-way, and foot-path:
25 poor Tom hath been scar'd out of his good wits. Bless
thee good man's son, from the foul Fiend. [Five fiends
have been in poor Tom at once; of lust, as Obidicut,
Hobbididance Prince of dumbness, Mahu of stealing,
Modo of murder, Flibbertigibbet of mopping and mow-
30   ing who since possesses chambermaids and waiting-wo-
men, so, bless thee, master.]

GLOUCESTER: Here take this purse, you whom the heavens' plagues

Have humbled to all strokes: that I am wretched
Makes thee happier: Heavens deal so still:
Let the superflous, and lust-dieted man,
That slaves your ordinance, that will not see
Because he does not feel, feel your power quickly: 5
So distribution should undo excess,
And each man have enough, Dost thou know Dover?
EDGAR: Ay master.
GLOUCESTER: There is a cliff, whose high and bending
    head   10
Looks fearfully in the confined deep:
Bring me but to the very brim of it,
And I'll repair the misery thou dost bear
With something rich about me: from that place,
I shall no leading need.   15
EDGAR: Give me thy arm;
Poor Tom shall lead thee.
                    Exeunt.

IV. 2

Enter Goneril, Bastard, and Steward.   20
GONERIL: Welcome my Lord. I marvel our mild husband
    Not met us on the way. Now, where's your master?
STEWARD: Madam within, but never man so chang'd:
I told him of the army that was landed:
He smil'd at it. I told him you were coming,   25
His answer was, the worse. Of Gloucester's treachery,
And of the loyal service of his son
When I inform'd him, then he call'd me sot.
And told me I had turn'd the wrong side out:
What most he should dislike, seems pleasant to him;   30
What like, offensive.

GONERIL: Then shall you go no further.
It is the cowish terror of his spirit
That dares not undertake: he'll not feel wrongs
Which tie him to an answer: our wishes on the way
5   May prove effects. Back, Edmund to my brother,
Hasten his musters, and conduct his powers.
I must change names at home, and give the distaff
Into my husband's hands. This trusty servant
Shall pass between us: ere long you are like to hear
10   (If you dare venture in your own behalf)
A mistress's command. Wear this; spare speech,
Decline your head. This kiss, if it durst speak
Would stretch thy spirits up into the air:
Conceive, and fare thee well.

15 BASTARD: Yours in the ranks of death.

Exit.

GONERIL: My most dear Gloucester.
Oh, the difference of man, and man,
To thee a woman's services are due,
20   My fool usurps my body.

STEWARD: Madam, here comes my Lord.

Exit.

Enter Albany.

GONERIL: I have been worth the whistle.

25 ALBANY: O Goneril,
You are not worth the dust which the rude wind
Blows in your face. [I fear your disposition:
That nature which contemns i' th' origin
Cannot be border'd certain in itself;
30   She that herself will sliver and disbranch
From her material sap, perforce must wither,
And come to deadly use.

GONERIL: No more, the text is foolish.

ALBANY: Wisdom and goodness, to the vile seem vile,
    Filths savour but themselves, what have you done?
    Tigers, not daughters, what have you perform'd?
    A father, and a gracious aged man
    Whose reverence even the head-lugg'd bear would lick,   5
    Most barbarous, most degenerate have you madded.
    Could my good brother suffer you to do it?
    A man, a Prince, by him so benefited,
    If that the heavens do not their visible spirits
    Send quickly down to tame this vile offence,   10
    It will come,
    Humanity must perforce prey on itself
    Like monsters of the deep.]
GONERIL: Milk-liver'd man,
    That bear'st a cheek for blows, a head for wrongs,   15
    Who hast not in thy brows an eye discerning
    Thine honour, from thy suffering; [that not know'st,
    Fools do those villains pity who are punish'd
    Ere they have done their mischief, Where's thy drum?
    France spreads his banners in our noiseless land,   20
    With plumed helm, thy state begins to threat;
    Whilst thou a moral fool sit'st still and cries,
    Alack why does he so?]
ALBANY: See thyself devil:
    Proper deformity seems not in the Fiend   25
    So horrid as in woman.
GONERIL: O vain fool.
[ALBANY: Thou changed, and self-cover'd thing for shame
    Be-monster not thy feature, were't my fitness
    To let these hands obey my blood,   30
    They are apt enough to dislocate and tear
    Thy flesh and bones, howe'er thou art a fiend,
    A woman's shape doth shield thee.

GONERIL: Marry your manhood mew –]

Enter a Messenger.

[ALBANY: What news?]

MESSENGER: O my good Lord, the Duke of Cornwall's
5   dead,
    Slain by his servant, going to put out
    The other eye of Gloucester.

ALBANY: Gloucester's eyes.

MESSENGER: A servant that he bred, thrill'd with remorse,
10   Oppos'd against the act: bending his sword
    To his great master, who, thereat enrag'd,
    Flew on him, and amongst them fell'd him dead,
    But not without that harmful stroke, which since
    Hath pluck'd him after.

15 ALBANY: This shows you are above
    You Justices, that these our nether crimes
    So speedily can venge. But (O poor Gloucester)
    Lost he his other eye?

MESSENGER: Both, both, my Lord.
20   This letter Madam, craves a speedy answer:
    'Tis from your sister.

GONERIL: One way I like this well.
    But being widow, and my Gloucester with her,
    May all the building in my fancy pluck
25   Upon my hateful life. Another way
    The news is not so tart. I'll read, and answer.

Exit.

ALBANY: Where was his son, when they did take his
    eyes?

30 MESSENGER: Come with my Lady hither.

ALBANY: He is not here.

MESSENGER: No my good Lord, I met him back again.

ALBANY: Knows he the wickedness?

MESSENGER: Ay my good Lord: 'twas he inform'd against
     him
     And quit the house on purpose, that their punishment
     Might have the freer course.
ALBANY: Gloucester, I live   5
     To thank thee for the love thou show'dst the King,
     And to revenge thine eyes. Come hither friend,
     Tell me what more thou know'st.
                    Exeunt.

[IV. 3   10

Enter Kent and a Gentleman.

KENT: Why the King of France is so suddenly gone back,
     know you no reason?
GENTLEMAN: Something he left imperfect in the state,
     which since his coming forth is thought of, which im-   15
     ports to the Kingdom, so much fear and danger that his
     personal return was most required and necessary.
KENT: Who hath he left behind him, General?
GENTLEMAN: The Marshal of France Monsieur La Far.
KENT: Did your letters pierce the Queen to any demon-   20
     stration of grief?
GENTLEMAN: I say she took them, read them in my pres-
     ence,
     And now and then an ample tear trill'd down
     Her delicate cheek, it seem'd she was a Queen   25
     Over her passion, who most rebel-like,
     Sought to be King o'er her.
KENT: O then it moved her.
GENTLEMAN: Not to a rage, patience and sorrow strove
     Who should express her goodliest, you have seen   30
     Sunshine and rain at once, her smiles and tears,

Were like a better way: those happy smilets,
That play'd on her ripe lip seem'd not to know,
What guests were in her eyes which parted thence,
As pearls from diamonds dropp'd; in brief,
5   Sorrow would be a rarity most beloved,
If all could so become it.

KENT: Made she no verbal question?

GENTLEMAN: 'Faith once or twice she heav'd the name of father,
10   Pantingly forth as if it press'd her heart,
Cried sisters, sisters, shame of Ladies, sisters:
Kent, father, sisters, what i' th' storm i' th' night;
Let pity not be believ'd, there she shook
The holy water from her heavenly eyes,
15   And clamour moisten'd her; then away she started,
To deal with grief alone.

KENT: It is the stars,
The stars above us govern our conditions,
Else one self mate and mate could not beget,
20   Such different issues. You spoke not with her since?

GENTLEMAN: No.

KENT: Was this before the King return'd?

GENTLEMAN: No, since.

KENT: Well sir, the poor distressed Lear's i' th' town,
25   Who sometime in his better tune remembers,
What we are come about, and by no means
Will yield to see his daughter.

GENTLEMAN: Why good sir?

KENT: A sovereign shame so elbows him; his own unkind-
30   ness
That stripp'd her from his benediction, turn'd her,
To foreign casualties, gave her dear rights
To his dog-hearted daughters, these things sting

His mind, so venomously that burning shame
Detains him from Cordelia.
GENTLEMAN: Alack poor gentleman.
KENT: Of Albany's and Cornwall's powers you heard not?
GENTLEMAN: 'Tis so they are afoot.   5
KENT: Well sir, I'll bring you to our master Lear,
And leave you to attend him: some dear cause
Will in concealment wrap me up awhile;
When I am known aright you shall not grieve,
Lending me this acquaintance. I pray you go   10
Along with me.

Exeunt.]

IV.4

*Enter with drum and colours, Cordelia, Gentleman and
Soldiers.*   15
CORDELIA: Alack, 'tis he: why he was met even now
As mad as the vex'd sea, singing aloud,
Crown'd with rank fumiter and furrow-weeds,
With bur-docks, hemlock, nettles, cuckoo-flowers,
Darnel, and all the idle weeds that grow   20
In our sustaining corn. A century send forth;
Search every acre in the high-grown field,
And bring him to our eye. What can man's wisdom
In the restoring his bereaved sense?
He that helps him, take all my outward worth.   25
GENTLEMAN: There is means, Madam:
Our foster-nurse of Nature, is repose,
The which he lacks: that to provoke in him
Are many simples operative, whose power
Will close the eye of anguish.   30
CORDELIA: All blest secrets,

All you unpublish'd virtues of the earth
Spring with my tears; be aidant, and remediate
In the good man's distress: seek, seek for him,
Lest his ungovern'd rage, dissolve the life
5 That wants the means to lead it.

Enter Messenger.

MESSENGER: News Madam,
The British powers are marching hitherward.

CORDELIA: 'Tis known before. Our preparation stands
10 In expectation of them. O dear father,
It is thy business that I go about: therefore great France
My mourning, and importune tears hath pitied:
No blown ambition doth our arms incite,
But love, dear love, and our ag'd father's right:
15 Soon may I hear, and see him.

Exeunt.

IV. 5

Enter Regan and Steward.

REGAN: But are my brother's powers set forth?
20 STEWARD: Ay Madam.
REGAN: Himself in person there?
STEWARD: Madam with much ado:
Your sister is the better soldier.
REGAN: Lord Edmund spake not with your Lord at home?
25 STEWARD: No Madam.
REGAN: What might import my sister's letter to him?
STEWARD: I know not, Lady.
REGAN: 'Faith he is posted hence on serious matter:
It was great ignorance, Gloucester's eyes being out
30 To let him live. Where he arrives, he moves
All hearts against us: Edmund, I think is gone

In pity of his misery, to dispatch
His nighted life: moreover to descry
The strength o' th' enemy.
STEWARD: I must needs after him, Madam, with my letter.
REGAN: Our troops set forth to-morrow, stay with us: 5
The ways are dangerous.
STEWARD: I may not Madam:
My Lady charg'd my duty in this business.
REGAN: Why should she write to Edmund? Might not you
Transport her purposes by word? Belike,   10
Some things, I know not what. I'll love thee much
Let me unseal the letter.
STEWARD: Madam, I had rather –
REGAN: I know your Lady does not love her husband,
I am sure of that: and at her late being here,   15
She gave strange œillades, and most speaking looks
To noble Edmund. I know you are of her bosom.
STEWARD: I, Madam?
REGAN: I speak in understanding: you are: I know't;
Therefore I do advise you take this note: 20
My Lord is dead: Edmund, and I have talk'd,
And more convenient is he for my hand
Than for your Lady's: you may gather more:
If you do find him, pray you give him this;
And when your mistress hears thus much from you,   25
I pray desire her call her wisdom to her.
So fare you well:
If you do chance to hear of that blind traitor,
Preferment falls on him, that cuts him off.
STEWARD: Would I could meet him Madam, I should show   30
What party I do follow.
REGAN: Fare thee well.

Exeunt.

IV.6

Enter Gloucester, and Edgar.

GLOUCESTER: When shall I come to th' top of that same
hill?

5 EDGAR: You do climb up it now. Look how we labour.

GLOUCESTER: Methinks the ground is even.

EDGAR: Horrible steep.
Hark, do you hear the sea?

GLOUCESTER: No truly.

10 EDGAR: Why then your other senses grow imperfect
By your eyes' anguish.

GLOUCESTER: So may it be indeed.
Methinks thy voice is alter'd, and thou speak'st
In better phrase, and matter than thou didst.

15 EDGAR: You are much deceiv'd: in nothing am I chang'd
But in my garments.

GLOUCESTER: Methinks you are better spoken.

EDGAR: Come on sir, here's the place: stand still: how
fearful

20 And dizzy 'tis, to cast one's eyes so low,
The crows and choughs, that wing the midway air
Show scarce so gross as beetles. Half way down
Hangs one that gathers samphire: dreadful trade:
Methinks he seems no bigger than his head.

25 The fishermen, that walk'd upon the beach
Appear like mice: and yond tall anchoring bark,
Diminish'd to her cock; her cock, a buoy
Almost too small for sight. The murmuring surge,
That on th' unnumber'd idle pebble chafes

30 Cannot be heard so high. I'll look no more,

Lest my brain turn, and the deficient sight
Topple down headlong.

GLOUCESTER: Set me where you stand.

EDGAR: Give me your hand:
You are now within a foot of th' extreme verge: 5
For all beneath the moon would I not leap upright.

GLOUCESTER: Let go my hand:
Here friend 's another purse: in it, a jewel
Well worth a poor man's taking. Fairies, and Gods
Prosper it with thee. Go thou further off, 10
Bid me farewell, and let me hear thee going.

EDGAR: Now fare you well, good sir.

GLOUCESTER: With all my heart.

EDGAR: Why I do trifle thus with his despair,
Is done to cure it. 15

He kneels.

GLOUCESTER: O you mighty Gods!
This world I do renounce, and in your sights
Shake patiently my great affliction off:
If I could bear it longer, and not fall
To quarrel with your great opposeless wills, 20
My snuff, and loathed part of Nature should
Burn itself out. If Edgar live, O bless him:
Now fellow, fare thee well.

He falls. 25

EDGAR: Gone sir, farewell:
And yet I know not how conceit may rob
The treasury of life, when life itself
Yields to the theft. Had he been where he thought,
By this had thought been past. Alive, or dead? 30
Hoa, you sir: friend, hear you sir, speak:
Thus might he pass indeed: yet he revives.
What are you sir?

GLOUCESTER: Away, and let me die.

EDGAR: Hadst thou been aught but gossamer, feathers, air,
(So many fathom down precipitating)
Thou'dst shiver'd like an egg: but thou dost breathe:
5   Hast heavy substance, bleed'st not, speak'st, art sound.
Ten masts at each, make not the altitude
Which thou hast perpendicularly fell,
Thy life's a miracle. Speak yet again.

GLOUCESTER: But have I fall'n, or no?

10 EDGAR: From the dread summit of this chalky bourn
Look up a height, the shrill-gorg'd lark so far
Cannot be seen, or heard: do but look up.

GLOUCESTER: Alack, I have no eyes:
Is wretchedness depriv'd that benefit
15   To end itself by death? 'Twas yet some comfort,
When misery could beguile the tyrant's rage,
And frustrate his proud will.

EDGAR: Give me your arm.
Up, so: how is't? Feel you your legs? You stand.

20 GLOUCESTER: Too well, too well.

EDGAR: This is above all strangeness.
Upon the crown o' th' cliff, what thing was that
Which parted from you?

GLOUCESTER: A poor unfortunate beggar.

25 EDGAR: As I stood here below, methought his eyes
Were two full moons: he had a thousand noses,
Horns whelk'd, and waved like the enraged sea:
It was some Fiend: therefore thou happy father,
Think that the clearest Gods, who make them honours
30   Of men's impossibilities, have preserved thee.

GLOUCESTER: I do remember now: henceforth I'll bear
Affliction, till it do cry out itself
Enough, enough, and die. That thing you speak of,

I took it for a man: often 'twould say
The Fiend, the Fiend; he led me to that place.

EDGAR: Bear free and patient thoughts.

Enter Lear, mad.

But who comes here?   5
The safer sense will ne'er accommodate
His master thus.

LEAR: No, they cannot touch me for coining. I am the
King himself.

EDGAR: O thou side-piercing sight!   10

LEAR: Nature's above Art, in that respect. There's your
press-money. That fellow handles his bow, like a crow-
keeper: draw me a clothier's yard. Look, look, a mouse:
peace, peace, this piece of toasted cheese will do't. There's
my gauntlet, I'll prove it on a giant. Bring up the brown   15
bills. O well flown bird: i' th' clout, i' th' clout: hewgh.
Give the word.

EDGAR: Sweet marjoram.

LEAR: Pass.

GLOUCESTER: I know that voice.   20

LEAR: Ha! Goneril with a white beard? They flatter'd me
like a dog, and told me I had the white hairs in my beard,
ere the black ones were there. To say ay, and no, to every
thing that I said: ay, and no too, was no good divinity.
When the rain came to wet me once, and the wind to   25
make me chatter: when the thunder would not peace at
my bidding, there I found 'em, there I smelt 'em out. Go
to, they are not men o' their words; they told me, I was
every thing: 'tis a lie, I am not ague-proof.

GLOUCESTER: The trick of that voice, I do well remember: 30
Is't not the King?

LEAR: Ay, every inch a King. When I do stare, see how
the subject quakes. I pardon that man's life. What was

thy cause? Adultery? Thou shalt not die: die for adultery? No, the wren goes to't, and the small gilded fly does lecher in my sight. Let copulation thrive: for Gloucester's bastard son was kinder to his father, than my daughters
5   got 'tween the lawful sheets. To't Luxury pell-mell, for I lack soldiers. Behold yond simpering dame, whose face between her forks presages snow; that minces virtue, and does shake the head to hear of pleasure's name. The fitchew, nor the soiled horse goes to't with a more riotous
10   appetite. Down from the waist they are Centaurs, though women all above: but to the girdle do the gods inherit, beneath is all the Fiends. There's hell, there's darkness, there is the sulphurous pit; burning, scalding, stench, consumption: fie, fie, fie; pah, pah: give me an ounce of
15   civet; good apothecary sweeten my imagination: there's money for thee.

GLOUCESTER: O let me kiss that hand.

LEAR: Let me wipe it first, it smells of mortality.

GLOUCESTER: O ruin'd piece of Nature, this great world
20   Shall so wear out to nought. Dost thou know me?

LEAR: I remember thine eyes well enough: dost thou squiny at me? No, do thy worst blind Cupid, I'll not love. Read thou this challenge, mark but the penning of it.

GLOUCESTER: Were all thy letters suns, I could not see.

25 EDGAR: I would not take this from report, it is,
And my heart breaks at it.

LEAR: Read.

GLOUCESTER: What with the case of eyes?

LEAR: Oh ho, are you there with me? No eyes in your
30   head, nor no money in your purse? Your eyes are in a heavy case, your purse in a light, yet you see how this world goes.

GLOUCESTER: I see it feelingly.

LEAR: What, art mad? A man may see how this world
goes, with no eyes. Look with thine ears: see how yond
Justice rails upon yond simple thief. Hark in thine ear:
change places, and handy-dandy, which is the Justice,
which is the thief: thou hast seen a farmer's dog bark at a 5
beggar?

GLOUCESTER: Ay sir.

LEAR: And the creature run from the cur: there thou
mightst behold the great image of authority, a dog's
obey'd in office. Thou, rascal beadle, hold thy bloody 10
hand: why dost thou lash that whore? Strip thy own
back, thou hotly lust'st to use her in that kind, for which
thou whipp'st her. The usurer hangs the cozener. Through
rough tatter'd clothes great vices do appear: robes, and
furr'd gowns hide all. Plate sins with gold, and the strong 15
lance of Justice, hurtless breaks: arm it in rags, a pigmy's
straw does pierce it. None does offend, none, I say none,
I'll able 'em; take that of me my friend, who have the
power to seal th' accuser's lips. Get thee glass-eyes, and
like a scurvy politician, seem to see the things thou dost 20
not. Now, now, now, now. Pull off my boots: harder,
harder, so.

EDGAR: O matter, and impertinency mix'd,
Reason in madness.

LEAR: If thou wilt weep my fortunes, take my eyes. 25
I know thee well enough, thy name is Gloucester:
Thou must be patient; we came crying hither:
Thou know'st, the first time that we smell the air
We wawl, and cry. I will preach to thee: mark.

GLOUCESTER: Alack, alack the day. 30

LEAR: When we are born, we cry that we are come
To this great stage of fools. This' a good block:
It were a delicate stratagem to shoe

A troop of horse with felt: I'll put't in proof,
And when I have stol'n upon these son-in-laws,
Then kill, kill, kill, kill, kill, kill.

Enter a Gentleman.

5 GENTLEMAN: O here he is: lay hand upon him, sir.
Your most dear daughter –

LEAR: No rescue? What, a prisoner? I am even
The natural fool of Fortune. Use me well,
You shall have ransom. Let me have surgeons,
10 I am cut to th' brains.

GENTLEMAN: You shall have any thing.

LEAR: No seconds? All myself?
Why, this would make a man, a man of salt
To use his eyes for garden water-pots,
15 [Ay and laying autumn's dust.]
I will die bravely, like a smug bridegroom. What?
I will be jovial: come, come, I am a King,
My masters, know you that?

GENTLEMAN: You are a royal one, and we obey you.

20 LEAR: Then there's life in't. Come, and you get it, you
shall get it running: sa, sa, sa, sa.

Exit Lear running.

GENTLEMAN: A sight most pitiful in the meanest wretch,
Past speaking of in a King. Thou hast a daughter
25 Who redeems Nature from the general curse
Which twain have brought her to.

EDGAR: Hail gentle sir.

GENTLEMAN: Sir, speed you: what's your will?

EDGAR: Do you hear aught, sir, of a battle toward?

30 GENTLEMAN: Most sure, and vulgar: every one hears that,
Which can distinguish sound.

EDGAR: But by your favour:
How near's the other army?

GENTLEMAN: Near, and on speedy foot: the main descry
  Stands on the hourly thought.

EDGAR: I thank you sir, that's all.

GENTLEMAN: Though that the Queen on special cause is
  here,   5
  Her army is mov'd on.

EDGAR: I thank you sir.

Exit Gentleman.

GLOUCESTER: You ever-gentle Gods, take my breath
  from me,   10
  Let not my worser spirit tempt me again
  To die before you please.

EDGAR: Well pray you father.

GLOUCESTER: Now good sir, what are you?

EDGAR: A most poor man, made tame to Fortune's blows 15
  Who, by the art of known, and feeling sorrows,
  Am pregnant to good pity. Give me your hand,
  I'll lead you to some biding.

GLOUCESTER: Hearty thanks:
  The bounty, and the benison of Heaven   20
  To boot, and boot.

Enter Steward.

STEWARD: A proclaim'd prize: most happy
  That eyeless head of thine, was first fram'd flesh
  To raise my fortunes. Thou old, unhappy traitor,   25
  Briefly thy self remember: the sword is out
  That must destroy thee.

GLOUCESTER: Now let thy friendly hand
  Put strength enough to't.

STEWARD: Wherefore, bold peasant,   30
  Dar'st thou support a publish'd traitor? Hence,
  Lest that th' infection of his fortune take
  Like hold on thee. Let go his arm.

EDGAR: Chill not let go zir, without vurther 'casion.

STEWARD: Let go slave, or thou diest.

EDGAR: Good gentleman go your gait, and let poor volk
pass: and 'chud ha' bin zwagger'd out of my life, 'twould
not ha' bin zo long as 'tis, by a vortnight. Nay, come not
near th' old man: keep out che vor' ye, or ise try whether
your costard, or my ballow be the harder; chill be plain
with you.

STEWARD: Out dunghill.

They fight.

EDGAR: Chill pick your teeth zir: come, no matter vor
your foins.

STEWARD: Slave thou hast slain me: villain, take my
purse;
If ever thou wilt thrive, bury my body,
And give the letters which thou find'st about me,
To Edmund Earl of Gloucester: seek him out
Upon the English party. O untimely death, death.

Dies.

EDGAR: I know thee well. A serviceable villain,
As duteous to the vices of thy Mistress,
As badness would desire.

GLOUCESTER: What, is he dead?

EDGAR: Sit you down father: rest you.
Let's see these pockets; the letters that he speaks of
May be my friends: he's dead; I am only sorry
He had no other death's-man. Let us see:
Leave gentle wax, and manners: blame us not
To know our enemies' minds, we rip their hearts,
Their papers is more lawful.

Reads the letter.

Let our reciprocal vows be remember'd. You have many oppor-
tunities to cut him off: if your will want not, time and place

*will be fruitfully offer'd. There is nothing done. If he return the
conqueror, then am I the prisoner, and his bed, my gaol, from
the loathed warmth whereof, deliver me, and supply the place
for your labour.*

> *Your (wife, so I would say)* 5
> *Affectionate servant,*
>
> GONERIL.

O undistinguish'd space of woman's will,
A plot upon her virtuous husband's life,
And the exchange my brother: here in the sands, 10
Thee I'll rake up, the post unsanctified
Of murtherous lechers: and in the mature time,
With this ungracious paper strike the sight
Of the death-practis'd Duke: for him 'tis well,
That of thy death, and business, I can tell. 15
GLOUCESTER: The King is mad: how stiff is my vile sense
That I stand up, and have ingenious feeling
Of my huge sorrows? Better I were distract,
So should my thoughts be sever'd from my griefs,

> *Drum afar off.* 20

And woes, by wrong imaginations lose
The knowledge of themselves.
EDGAR: Give me your hand:
Far off methinks I heard the beaten drum.
Come father, I'll bestow you with a friend. 25

> *Exeunt.*

IV.7

Enter Cordelia, Kent, and Doctor.
CORDELIA: O thou good Kent, how shall I live and work
To match thy goodness? My life will be too short, 30
And every measure fail me.

KENT: To be acknowledg'd Madam is o'erpaid,
All my reports go with the modest truth,
Nor more, nor clipp'd, but so.

CORDELIA: Be better suited;
5   These weeds are memories of those worser hours:
I prithee put them off.

KENT: Pardon dear Madam,
Yet to be known shortens my made intent,
My boon I make it, that you know me not,
10   Till time and I, think meet.

CORDELIA: Then be 't so my good Lord: how does the King?

DOCTOR: Madam sleeps still.

CORDELIA: O you kind Gods!
15   Cure this great breach in his abused Nature,
Th' untun'd and jarring senses, O wind up,
Of this child-changed father.

DOCTOR: So please your Majesty,
That we may wake the King, he hath slept long.

20 **CORDELIA:** Be govern'd by your knowledge, and proceed
I' th' sway of your own will: is he array'd?

Enter Lear in a chair carried by servants.

DOCTOR: Ay Madam: in the heaviness of sleep,
We put fresh garments on him.
25   Be by good Madam when we do awake him,
I doubt of his temperance.

[**CORDELIA:** Very well.

DOCTOR: Please you draw near, louder the music there.]

30 **CORDELIA:** O my dear father, restoration hang
Thy medicine on my lips, and let this kiss
Repair those violent harms, that my two sisters
Have in thy reverence made.

KENT: Kind and dear Princess.

CORDELIA: Had you not been their father, these white
flakes
Did challenge pity of them. Was this a face
To be oppos'd against the jarring winds?   5
[To stand against the deep dread-bolted thunder?
In the most terrible and nimble stroke
Of quick cross lightning, to watch *poor perdu*
With this thin helm?] Mine enemy's dog,
Though he had bit me, should have stood that night   10
Against my fire, and wast thou fain, poor father,
To hovel thee with swine and rogues forlorn,
In short, and musty straw? Alack, alack,
'Tis wonder that thy life and wits, at once
Had not concluded all. He wakes, speak to him.   15

DOCTOR: Madam do you, 'tis fittest.

CORDELIA: How does my royal Lord? How fares your
Majesty?

LEAR: You do me wrong to take me out o' th' grave,
Thou art a soul in bliss, but I am bound   20
Upon a wheel of fire, that mine own tears
Do scald, like molten lead.

CORDELIA: Sir, do you know me?

LEAR: You are a spirit I know, where did you die?

CORDELIA: Still, still, far wide.   25

DOCTOR: He's scarce awake, let him alone awhile.

LEAR: Where have I been? Where am I? Fair daylight?
I am mightily abus'd; I should e'en die with pity
To see another thus. I know not what to say:
I will not swear these are my hands: let's see,   30
I feel this pin prick, would I were assur'd
Of my condition.

CORDELIA: O look upon me sir,

And hold your hand in benediction o'er me,
You must not kneel.

LEAR: Pray do not mock me:
I am a very foolish fond old man,
5   Fourscore and upward, not an hour more, nor less:
And to deal plainly,
I fear I am not in my perfect mind.
Methinks I should know you, and know this man,
Yet I am doubtful: for I am mainly ignorant
10   What place this is: and all the skill I have
Remembers not these garments: nor I know not
Where I did lodge last night. Do not laugh at me,
For, as I am a man, I think this Lady
To be my child Cordelia.

15 CORDELIA: And so I am: I am.

LEAR: Be your tears wet? yes 'faith: I pray weep not;
If you have poison for me, I will drink it:
I know you do not love me, for your sisters
Have, as I do remember, done me wrong.
20   You have some cause, they have not.

CORDELIA: No cause, no cause.

LEAR: Am I in France?

KENT: In your own kingdom sir.

LEAR: Do not abuse me.

25 DOCTOR: Be comforted good Madam, the great rage
You see is kill'd in him: [and yet it is danger
To make him even o'er the time he has lost:]
Desire him to go in, trouble him no more
Till further settling.

30 CORDELIA: Will't please your Highness walk?

LEAR: You must bear with me:
Pray you now forget, and forgive, I am old and foolish.
        Exeunt all but Kent and Gentleman.

[GENTLEMAN: Holds it true sir, that the Duke of Cornwall was so slain?

KENT: Most certain sir.

GENTLEMAN: Who is conductor of his people?

KENT: As 'tis said, the bastard son of Gloucester.   5

GENTLEMAN: They say Edgar his banish'd son is with the
   Earl of Kent in Germany.

KENT: Report is changeable, 'tis time to look about, the
   powers of the kingdom approach apace.

GENTLEMAN: The arbitrement is like to be bloody, fare   10
   you well sir.

                    Exit.

KENT: My point and period will be throughly wrought,
   Or well, or ill, as this day's battle's fought.

                    Exit.]   15

V.1

Enter with drum and colours, Bastard, Regan,
Gentlemen, and Soldiers.

BASTARD: Know of the Duke if his last purpose hold,
   Or whether since he is advis'd by aught   20
   To change the course; he's full of alteration,
   And self-reproving; bring his constant pleasure.

REGAN: Our sister's man is certainly miscarried.

BASTARD: 'Tis to be doubted Madam.

REGAN: Now sweet Lord,   25
   You know the goodness I intend upon you:
   Tell me but truly, but then speak the truth,
   Do you not love my sister?

BASTARD: In honour'd love.

REGAN: But have you never found my brother's way,   30
   To the for-fended place?

[BASTARD: That thought abuses you.

REGAN: I am doubtful that you have been conjunct
And bosom'd with her, as far as we call hers.]

BASTARD: No by mine honour, Madam.

5 REGAN: I never shall endure her, dear my Lord
Be not familiar with her.

BASTARD: Fear not, she and the Duke her husband.

Enter with drum and colours, Albany, Goneril,
Soldiers.

10 [GONERIL: I had rather lose the battle than that sister
Should loosen him and me.]

ALBANY: Our very loving sister, well be-met:
Sir, this I heard, the King is come to his daughter
With others, whom the rigour of our state

15 Forc'd to cry out: [Where I could not be honest
I never yet was valiant, for this business
It touches us, as France invades our land,
Not bolds the King, with others whom I fear,
Most just and heavy causes make oppose.

20 BASTARD: Sir you speak nobly.]

REGAN: Why is this reason'd?

GONERIL: Combine together 'gainst the enemy:
For these domestic and particular broils,
Are not the question here.

25 ALBANY: Let's then determine
With th' ancient of war on our proceeding.

[BASTARD: I shall attend you presently at your tent.]

REGAN: Sister you'll go with us?

GONERIL: No.

30 REGAN: 'Tis most convenient, pray go with us.

GONERIL: Oh ho, I know the riddle, I will go.

Exeunt both the armies.

Enter Edgar.

EDGAR: If e'er your Grace had speech with man so poor,
    Hear me one word.
ALBANY: I'll overtake you, speak.
EDGAR: Before you fight the battle, ope this letter:
    If you have victory, let the trumpet sound   5
    For him that brought it: wretched though I seem,
    I can produce a champion, that will prove
    What is avouched there. If you miscarry,
    Your business of the world hath so an end,
    And machination ceases. Fortune loves you.   10
ALBANY: Stay till I have read the letter.
EDGAR: I was forbid it:
    When time shall serve, let but the herald cry,
    And I'll appear again.

                        Exit.   15

ALBANY: Why fare thee well, I will o'erlook thy paper.

                Enter Bastard.

BASTARD: The enemy's in view, draw up your powers,
    Here is the guess of their true strength and forces,
    By diligent discovery, but your haste   20
    Is now urg'd on you.
ALBANY: We will greet the time.

                        Exit.

BASTARD: To both these sisters have I sworn my love;
    Each jealous of the other, as the stung   25
    Are of the adder. Which of them shall I take?
    Both? One? Or neither? Neither can be enjoy'd
    If both remain alive: to take the widow,
    Exasperates, makes mad her sister Goneril,
    And hardly shall I carry out my side,   30
    Her husband being alive. Now then, we'll use
    His countenance for the battle, which being done,
    Let her who would be rid of him, devise

His speedy taking off. As for the mercy
Which he intends to Lear and to Cordelia,
The battle done, and they within our power,
Shall never see his pardon: for my state,
5 Stands on me to defend, not to debate.

Exit.

V.2

*Alarum within. Enter with drum and colours, Lear, Cordelia,
and Soldiers over the stage, and exeunt.*
10   *Enter Edgar, and Gloucester.*

EDGAR: Here father, take the shadow of this tree
For your good host: pray that the right may thrive:
If ever I return to you again,
I'll bring you comfort.

15 GLOUCESTER: Grace go with you sir.

Exit Edgar.

Alarum and retreat within. Enter Edgar.

EDGAR: Away old man, give me thy hand, away:
King Lear hath lost, he and his daughter ta'en;
20 Give me thy hand: come on.

GLOUCESTER: No further sir, a man may rot even here.

EDGAR: What in ill thoughts again?
Men must endure
Their going hence, even as their coming hither,
25 Ripeness is all: come on.

GLOUCESTER: And that's true too.

Exeunt.

V. 3

Enter in conquest with drum and colours, Bastard, Lear and
Cordelia, as prisoners, Soldiers, Captain.

BASTARD: Some officers take them away: good guard,
　Until their greater pleasures first be known   5
　That are to censure them.
CORDELIA: We are not the first,
　Who with best meaning have incurr'd the worst:
　For thee oppressed King I am cast down,
　Myself could else out-frown false Fortune's frown.   10
　Shall we not see these daughters, and these sisters?
LEAR: No, no, no, no: come let's away to prison,
　We two alone will sing like birds i' th' cage:
　When thou dost ask me blessing, I'll kneel down
　And ask of thee forgiveness: so we'll live,   15
　And pray, and sing, and tell old tales, and laugh
　At gilded butterflies: and hear (poor rogues)
　Talk of Court news, and we'll talk with them too,
　Who loses, and who wins; who's in, who's out;
　And take upon's the mystery of things,   20
　As if we were God's spies: and we'll wear out
　In a wall'd prison, packs and sects of great ones,
　That ebb and flow by th' moon.
BASTARD: Take them away.
LEAR: Upon such sacrifices, my Cordelia,   25
　The Gods themselves throw incense. Have I caught thee?
　He that parts us, shall bring a brand from Heaven,
　And fire us hence, like foxes: wipe thine eyes,
　The good-years shall devour them, flesh and fell,
　Ere they shall make us weep: 30
　We'll see 'em starve first: come.
　　　　　Exeunt Lear and Cordelia, guarded.

BASTARD: Come hither Captain, hark.
Take thou this note, go follow them to prison,
One step I have advanc'd thee, if thou dost
As this instructs thee, thou dost make thy way
5   To noble fortunes: know thou this, that men
Are as the time is; to be tender minded
Does not become a sword, thy great employment
Will not bear question: either say thou'lt do't,
Or thrive by other means.
10 CAPTAIN: I'll do't my Lord.
BASTARD: About it, and write happy, when th' hast
done;
Mark I say instantly, and carry it so
As I have set it down.
15 [CAPTAIN: I cannot draw a cart, nor eat dried oats,
If it be man's work I'll do it.]
Exit.
Flourish. Enter Albany, Goneril, Regan, and Soldiers.
ALBANY: Sir, you have show'd to-day your valiant strain
20   And Fortune led you well: you have the captives
Who were the opposites of this day's strife:
I do require them of you so to use them,
As we shall find their merits, and our safety
May equally determine.
25 BASTARD: Sir, I thought it fit,
To send the old and miserable King to some reten-
tion:
Whose age has charms in it, whose title more,
To pluck the common bosom on his side,
30   And turn our impress'd lances in our eyes
Which do command them. With him I sent the Queen:
My reason all the same, and they are ready
To-morrow, or at further space, t' appear

Where you shall hold your session [at this time,
We sweat and bleed, the friend hath lost his friend,
And the best quarrels in the heat are curs'd,
By those that feel their sharpness;
The question of Cordelia and her father 5
Requires a fitter place.]

ALBANY: Sir, by your patience,
I hold you but a subject of this war,
Not as a brother.

REGAN: That's as we list to grace him. 10
Methinks our pleasure might have been demanded
Ere you had spoke so far. He led our powers,
Bore the commission of my place and person,
The which immediacy may well stand up,
And call itself your brother. 15

GONERIL: Not so hot:
In his own grace he doth exalt himself,
More than in your addition.

REGAN: In my rights,
By me invested, he compeers the best. 20

GONERIL: That were the most, if he should husband you.

REGAN: Jesters do oft prove prophets.

GONERIL: Hola, hola,
That eye that told you so, look'd but a-squint.

REGAN: Lady I am not well, else I should answer 25
From a full-flowing stomach. General,
Take thou my soldiers, prisoners, patrimony,
Dispose of them, of me, the walls is thine:
Witness the world, that I create thee here
My Lord, and master. 30

GONERIL: Mean you to enjoy him?

ALBANY: The let-alone lies not in your good will.

BASTARD: Nor in thine, Lord.

ALBANY: Half-blooded fellow, yes.

REGAN: Let the drum strike, and prove my title thine.

ALBANY: Stay yet, hear reason: Edmund, I arrest thee
On capital treason; and in thy arrest,
5   This gilded serpent; for your claim fair sister,
I bar it in the interest of my wife,
'Tis she is sub-contracted to this Lord,
And I her husband contradict your banns.
If you will marry, make your loves to me,
10   My Lady is bespoke.

GONERIL: An interlude.

ALBANY: Thou art arm'd Gloucester, let the trumpet sound:
If none appear to prove upon thy person,
Thy heinous, manifest, and many treasons,
15   There is my pledge: I'll make it on thy heart
Ere I taste bread, thou art in nothing less
Than I have here proclaim'd thee.

REGAN: Sick, O sick.

GONERIL: If not, I'll ne'er trust medicine.

20 BASTARD: There's my exchange, what in the world he is
That names me traitor, villain-like he lies,
Call by the trumpet: he that dares approach;
On him, on you, who not, I will maintain
My truth and honour firmly.

25   *Enter a herald.*

ALBANY: A herald, ho.

BASTARD: [A herald, ho, a herald.]

ALBANY: Trust to thy single virtue, for thy soldiers
All levied in my name, have in my name
30   Took their discharge.

REGAN: My sickness grows upon me.

ALBANY: She is not well, convey her to my tent.

                        Exit Regan, led.

Come hither herald, let the trumpet sound,
And read out this.

A trumpet sounds.

Herald reads.

If any man of quality or degree, within the lists of the army,   5
will maintain upon Edmund, supposed Earl of Gloucester, that
he is a manifold traitor, let him appear by the third sound of
the Trumpet: he is bold in his defence.

BASTARD: Sound.

First trumpet.   10

HERALD: Again.

Second trumpet.

HERALD: Again.

Third trumpet.

Trumpet answers within.   15

Enter Edgar, at the third sound, armed, with a trumpet before
him.

ALBANY: Ask him his purposes, why he appears
Upon this call o' th' trumpet.

HERALD: What are you?   20
Your name, your quality, and why you answer
This present summons?

EDGAR: Know my name is lost
By treason's tooth: bare-gnawn, and canker-bit;
Yet am I noble as the adversary   25
I come to cope.

ALBANY: Which is that adversary?

EDGAR: What's he that speaks for Edmund Earl of Gloucester?

BASTARD: Himself, what say'st thou to him?   30

EDGAR: Draw thy sword,
That if my speech offend a noble heart,

Thy arm may do thee justice, here is mine:
Behold it is my privilege,
The privilege of mine honour,
My oath, and my profession. I protest,
5 Maugre thy strength, place, youth, and eminence,
Despite thy victor-sword, and fire new Fortune,
Thy valour, and thy heart, thou art a traitor:
False to thy Gods, thy brother, and thy father,
Conspirant 'gainst this high-illustrious Prince,
10 And from th' extremest upward of thy head,
To the descent and dust below thy foot,
A most toad-spotted traitor. Say thou no,
This sword, this arm, and my best spirits are bent
To prove upon thy heart, whereto I speak,
15 Thou liest.

BASTARD: In wisdom I should ask thy name,
But since thy outside looks so fair and warlike,
And that thy tongue (some say) of breeding breathes,
What safe, and nicely I might well delay,
20 By rule of knighthood, I disdain and spurn:
Back do I toss these treasons to thy head,
With the hell-hated lie o'erwhelm thy heart,
Which for they yet glance by, and scarcely bruise,
This sword of mine shall give them instant way,
25 Where they shall rest for ever. Trumpets speak.
              Alarums. They fight. Bastard falls.

ALBANY: Save him, save him.

GONERIL: This is practice Gloucester,
By th' Law of War, thou wast not bound to answer
30 An unknown opposite; thou art not vanquish'd,
But cozen'd and beguil'd.

ALBANY: Shut your mouth Dame,
Or with this paper shall I stop it: hold sir,

Thou worse than any name, read thine own evil:
No tearing Lady, I perceive you know it.

GONERIL: Say if I do, the Laws are mine not thine,
    Who can arraign me for't?

Exit.   5

ALBANY: Most monstrous! O, know'st thou this paper?

BASTARD: Ask me not what I know.

ALBANY: Go after her, she's desperate, govern her.

BASTARD: What you have charg'd me with, that have I
    done,   10
    And more, much more, the time will bring it out.
    'Tis past, and so am I: but what art thou
    That hast this fortune on me? If thou 'rt noble,
    I do forgive thee.

EDGAR: Let's exchange charity: 15
    I am no less in blood than thou art Edmund,
    If more, the more th' hast wrong'd me.
    My name is Edgar and thy father's son,
    The Gods are just, and of our pleasant vices
    Make instruments to plague us: 20
    The dark and vicious place where thee he got,
    Cost him his eyes.

BASTARD: Th' hast spoken right, 'tis true,
    The wheel is come full circle, I am here.

ALBANY: Methought thy very gait did prophesy   25
    A royal nobleness: I must embrace thee,
    Let sorrow split my heart, if ever I
    Did hate thee, or thy father.

EDGAR: Worthy Prince, I know't.

ALBANY: Where have you hid yourself?   30
    How have you known the miseries of your father?

EDGAR: By nursing them my Lord. List a brief tale,
    And when 'tis told, O that my heart would burst.

The bloody proclamation to escape
That follow'd me so near, (O our lives' sweetness,
That we the pain of death would hourly die,
Rather than die at once) taught me to shift
5   Into a madman's rags, t' assume a semblance
That very dogs disdain'd: and in this habit
Met I my father with his bleeding rings,
Their precious stones new lost: became his guide,
Led him, begg'd for him, sav'd him from despair.
10   Never (O fault) reveal'd myself unto him,
Until some half-hour past when I was arm'd,
Not sure, though hoping of this good success,
I ask'd his blessing, and from first to last
Told him our pilgrimage. But his flaw'd heart
15   (Alack too weak the conflict to support)
'Twixt two extremes of passion, joy and grief,
Burst smilingly.
  BASTARD: This speech of yours hath mov'd me,
And shall perchance do good, but speak you on,
20   You look as you had something more to say.
   ALBANY: If there be more, more woeful, hold it in,
For I am almost ready to dissolve,
Hearing of this.
  [EDGAR: This would have seem'd a period
25   To such as love not sorrow, but another
To amplify too much, would make much more,
And top extremity.
Whilst I was big in clamour, came there in a man,
Who having seen me in my worst estate,
30   Shunn'd my abhorr'd society, but then finding
Who 'twas that so endur'd, with his strong arms
He fasten'd on my neck and bellow'd out,
As he'ld burst heaven, threw him on my father,

Told the most piteous tale of Lear and him,
That ever ear receiv'd, which in recounting
His grief grew puissant and the strings of life,
Began to crack, twice then the trumpets sounded,
And there I left him tranc'd.   5

ALBANY: But who was this?

EDGAR: Kent sir, the banish'd Kent, who in disguise,
Follow'd his enemy king and did him service
Improper for a slave.]

       Enter a Gentleman, with a bloody knife.   10

GENTLEMAN: Help, help: O help.

EDGAR: What kind of help?

ALBANY: Speak man.

EDGAR: What means this bloody knife?

GENTLEMAN: 'Tis hot, it smokes, it came even from the   15
heart of – O she's dead.

ALBANY: Who dead? Speak man.

GENTLEMAN: Your Lady sir, your Lady; and her sister
By her is poison'd: she confesses it.

BASTARD: I was contracted to them both, all three   20
Now marry in an instant.

EDGAR: Here comes Kent.

       Enter Kent.

ALBANY: Produce the bodies, be they alive or dead;
This judgement of the Heavens that makes us trembie,   25
Touches us not with pity.
O, is this he?
The time will not allow the compliment
Which very manners urges.

KENT: I am come   30
To bid my King and master aye good night.
Is he not here?

ALBANY: Great thing of us forgot,

Speak Edmund, where's the King? and where's Cordelia?

See'st thou this object Kent?

The bodies of Goneril and Regan are brought in.

5 KENT: Alack, why thus?

BASTARD: Yet Edmund was belov'd:

The one the other poison'd for my sake,

And after slew herself.

ALBANY: Even so: cover their faces.

10 BASTARD: I pant for life: some good I mean to do

Despite of mine own Nature. Quickly send,

(Be brief in it) to th' Castle, for my writ

Is on the life of Lear and on Cordelia:

Nay, send in time.

15 ALBANY: Run, run, O run.

EDGAR: To who my Lord? Who has the office? send

Thy token of reprieve.

BASTARD: Well thought on, take my sword,

Give it the captain.

20 ALBANY: Haste thee for thy life.

Exit Gentleman.

BASTARD: He hath commission from thy wife and me,

To hang Cordelia in the prison, and

To lay the blame upon her own despair,

25 That she fordid herself.

ALBANY: The Gods defend her, bear him hence awhile.

Edmund is borne off.

Enter Lear with Cordelia in his arms.

LEAR: Howl, howl, howl: O you are men of stones,

30 Had I your tongues and eyes, I'ld use them so,

That Heaven's vault should crack: she's gone for ever.

I know when one is dead, and when one lives,

She's dead as earth: lend me a looking-glass,
If that her breath will mist or stain the stone,
Why then she lives.

KENT: Is this the promis'd end?

EDGAR: Or image of that horror? 5

ALBANY: Fall and cease.

LEAR: This feather stirs, she lives: if it be so,
It is a chance which does redeem all sorrows
That ever I have felt.

KENT: O my good master. 10

LEAR: Prithee away.

EDGAR: 'Tis noble Kent, your friend.

LEAR: A plague upon you murderers, traitors all,
I might have sav'd her, now she's gone for ever:
Cordelia, Cordelia, stay a little. Ha: 15
What is't thou say'st? Her voice was ever soft,
Gentle, and low, an excellent thing in woman.
I kill'd the slave that was a-hanging thee.

CAPTAIN: 'Tis true, my Lords, he did.

LEAR: Did I not fellow? 20
I have seen the day, with my good biting falchion
I would have made him skip: I am old now,
And these same crosses spoil me. Who are you?
Mine eyes are not o' th' best, I'll tell you straight.

KENT: If Fortune brag of two, she lov'd and hated, 25
One of them we behold.

LEAR: This is a dull sight, are you not Kent?

KENT: The same:
Your servant Kent, where is your servant Caius.

LEAR: He's a good fellow, I can tell you that, 30
He'll strike and quickly too, he's dead and rotten.

KENT: No my good Lord, I am the very man.

LEAR: I'll see that straight.

KENT: That from your first of difference and decay,
   Have follow'd your sad steps.

LEAR: You are welcome hither.

KENT: Nor no man else: all's cheerless, dark, and deadly,
5 Your eldest daughters have fordone themselves,
   And desperately are dead.

LEAR: Ay so I think.

ALBANY: He knows not what he says, and vain is it
   That we present us to him.

10 EDGAR: Very bootless.

Enter a Messenger.

MESSENGER: Edmund is dead my Lord.

ALBANY: That's but a trifle here:
   You Lords and noble friends, know our intent,
15 What comfort to this great decay may come,
   Shall be appli'd. For us we will resign,
   During the life of this old Majesty
   To him our absolute power, you to your rights,
   With boot, and such addition as your honours
20 Have more than merited. All friends shall taste
   The wages of their virtue, and all foes
   The cup of their deservings: O see, see.

LEAR: And my poor fool is hang'd: no, no, no life?
   Why should a dog, a horse, a rat have life,
25 And thou no breath at all? Thou'lt come no more,
   Never, never, never, never, never.
   Pray you undo this button. Thank you sir,
   Do you see this? Look on her? look her lips,
   Look there, look there.

30   *He dies.*

EDGAR: He faints, my Lord, my Lord.

KENT: Break heart, I prithee break.

EDGAR: Look up my Lord.

KENT: Vex not his ghost, O let him pass, he hates him,
  That would upon the rack of this tough world
  Stretch him out longer.

EDGAR: He is gone indeed.

KENT: The wonder is, he hath endur'd so long,   5
  He but usurp'd his life.

ALBANY: Bear them from hence, our present business
  Is general woe: friends of my soul, you twain,
  Rule in this Realm, and the gor'd state sustain.

KENT: I have a journey sir, shortly to go,   10
  My master calls me, I must not say no.

EDGAR: The weight of this sad time we must obey,
  Speak what we feel, not what we ought to say:
  The oldest hath borne most, we that are young,
  Shall never see so much, nor live so long.   15

  Exeunt with a dead march.

*

NOTES

*References are to the page and line of this edition;
a full page contains 33 lines.*

As the audience was familiar with the story, Shakespeare needed only to show at what point the play opens. Lear has already decided to divide the kingdom amongst his daughters; there remains only the public and ceremonious ratification.

P. 23 L. 7   *equalities ... moiety*: their shares are so equal that close examination [*curiosity*] cannot discover any inequality as between either share [*moiety*].

P. 24 L. 2   *study deserving*: do my best to deserve your favour. This stage direction, showing how the entry was made on the stage of the Globe Theatre, is from the Quarto.

P. 24 L. 12   *we shall express*: Lear as King on this formal occasion uses the royal 'We'.

P. 25 L. 20   *precious square of sense*: feeling in the highest degree.

P. 25 L. 20   *square*: the carpenter's rule, i.e. measurement.

P. 25 L. 30   *our last and least*: This is the Folio reading. The Quarto reads –

> but now our joy,
> Although the last, not least in our dear love,
> What can you say to win a third, more opulent
> Than your sisters?

P. 26 L. 1   *Nothing my Lord*: Cordelia's 'nothing' is subtle psychology. She suffers from that kind of paralysis of the will which sometimes overcomes those who are unwillingly forced to display their deepest affections in public. Whatever she might wish to say, all her tongue can frame is 'Nothing'. In *Lear* Shakespeare very deliberately used the words 'Nothing' and 'Nature' in all their possible meanings, as a kind of knell which tolls insistently throughout the play.

P. 26 L. 4   *Nothing will come of nothing*: the old philosopher's maxim of *ex nihilo nihil fit.* Lear is unconscious of the tremendous significance of the results of this 'nothing'; for out of Cordelia's 'nothing' comes everything.

P. 26 L. 7   *According ... bond:* i.e. the tie of natural affection.

P. 26 L. 27   *operation of the orbs:* influence of the planets.

P. 26 L. 32   *Scythian ... generation messes:* The Scythians, who lived in South Russia, were believed to eat their parents. 'Generation' means either 'parents' or (more usually) 'children'.

P. 27 L. 6   *Dragon:* the Dragon of Britain was Lear's heraldic device, and also a symbol of his ferocity.

P. 27 L. 7   *Set my rest:* an image from the game of primero, where it means lit. to risk all. Lear uses the phrase with the double meaning of find rest.

P. 27 L. 15   *large effects ... majesty:* outward shows that denote power.

P. 27 L. 32   *old man:* Kent too has lost his temper so completely that he addresses his King thus.

P. 28 L. 3   *reserve thy state:* keep your power. The Quarto reads 'reverse thy doom'.

P. 28 L. 10   *pawn:* a pledge to be sacrificed.

P. 28 L. 15   *blank:* centre, usually of a target, as in the modern 'bull's eye'.

P. 28 L. 25   *on thine allegiance:* The most solemn form of command which could be laid on a subject: to disobey was high treason.

P. 28 L. 30   *potency made good:* our power being thus re-established.

P. 29 L. 5   *Fare thee well ... new:* The rhyme used here and elsewhere in the play stiffens the speech and gives it a special prophetic or moral significance: e.g. p. 31 l. 22 – p. 32 l. 4 – p. 91 l. 23 – p. 92 l. 1.

P. 29 L. 29   *little seeming substance:* body which seems so small. That Cordelia is so little increases the offence in Lear's eyes: she is his 'last and least'.

P. 30 L. 6   *Election ... conditions:* i.e., one does not choose one's wife on such terms.

P. 31 L. 10   *intire point:* essential point, i.e. love.

P. 31 L. 20   *respect and Fortune:* i.e. my dowry.

P. 31 L. 27   *inflam'd respect:* hotter love.

P. 32 L. 9   *The jewels of our father ... named:* i.e. although our father regards you as his precious jewels yet I know what you are.

P. 32 L. 13   *professed:* which profess such affection.

P. 32 L. 20   *At Fortune's alms:* i.e. as a charitable gift.

P. 32 L. 21   *well are worth . . . wanted:* deserve the same lack of love which you have shown.

P. 32 L. 22   *plighted:* covered with folds (pleats).

P. 32 L. 28   *Sister, it is. ... :* The abrupt change from verse to prose marks the change from the emotion of the previous speeches to the cynical frankness of the two sisters.

P. 33 L. 8   *long-ingraffed condition:* i.e. the imperious temper which has long been part of his nature.

P. 33 L. 14   *if our father ... offend us:* i.e. if the King continues to have any real power he will be a nuisance.

P. 33 L. 22   *Thou Nature art my Goddess?* The 'natural' son naturally dedicates himself to Nature whose doctrine is every creature ruthlessly for itself.

P. 33 L. 25   *curiosity of Nations:* i.e. nice distinctions of the laws of Nations – between legitimate and illegitimate.

P. 34 L. 16   *Prescrib'd his power:* abdicated.

P. 34 L. 17   *Confin'd to exhibition:* reduced to a pension.

P. 34 L. 18   *Upon the gad:* as if suddenly pricked.

P. 34 L. 24   *Nothing my Lord:* see note on p. 26 l. 4. Gloucester's tragedy also begins with the word 'nothing'.

P. 36 L. 16   *auricular assurance:* proof heard with your ears.

P. 36 L. 24   *unstate ... resolution:* I would lose my Earldom to know for certain – as afterwards comes to pass.

P. 36 L. 28   *These late eclipses. ...* See Introduction p. 15.

P. 36 L. 29   *wisdom of Nature:* rational explanations.

P. 37 L. 10   *This is the excellent foppery. ...* This second soliloquy of Edmund is in prose, the first (p. 33 l. 22) in verse, which contrasts the passion of the first with the cynicism of the second speech. It is also a comment on contemporary credulity.

P. 37 L. 14   *treachers by spherical predominance:* i.e. traitors because the stars decreed so at our nativities.

P. 37 L. 18   *to lay ... star:* to blame some planet because he has the morals of a goat.

P. 37 L. 24   *Edgar ... catastrophe of the old comedy:* i.e., he arrives as conveniently as a character in an old-fashioned play.

P. 37 L. 26   *cue ... Tom o' Bedlam:* I must now pretend to be melancholic and sigh like a lunatic beggar. *Tom o' Bedlam:* a lunatic who had been let out of Bedlam (Bethlehem) Madhouse to wander about begging. These beggars were one of the terrors of the countryside. Edgar describes them on p. 64 l. 8.

P. 37 L. 28   *Fa, sol, la, mi:* i.e., he hums a few notes.

P. 38 L. 6   *dissipation of cohorts:* separation of united friends.

P. 38 L. 22   *continent forbearance:* patience which will keep you from rashness.

P. 39 L. 20   *come slack ... services:* i.e. do not wait on him so efficiently as before.

P. 39 L. 24   *come to question:* i.e. brought to a head.

P. 39 L. 30   *Old fools ... checks as flatteries:* i.e. old men must be treated like babies and checked when they are naughty.

P. 40 L. 7   *breed ... occasions:* find excuses for taking action.

P. 40 L. 15   *that full issue:* successfully.

P. 40 L. 24   *What ... profess?:* what is your profession?

P. 40 L. 29   *eat no fish:* i.e. no Catholic to respect fast days.

P. 41 L. 14   *mar a curious tale:* i.e. I'm not one to delight in elaborate tales. He will have none of the fantastic talk of the typical courtier (such as Osric in *Hamlet*), which he mimics at p. 61 l. 11.

P. 42 L. 8   *ceremonious affection:* Manners, even between parents and children, were very formal. Neglect of courtesies to the ex-King shows of falling off of love.

P. 43 L. 5   *I'll teach you differences:* i.e., of rank.

P. 43 L. 9   *earnest of thy service:* Lear gives him money as token that he is engaged.

P. 43 L. 12   *coxcomb:* the fool's cap, shaped like a cock's comb.

P. 43 L. 26 *Take heed sirrah, the whip:* The fool's profession was precarious, and in real life too smart a joke brought its reward. Thus, in March, 1605, Stone the Fool was well whipped in Bridewell for saying that 'there went sixty fools into Spain, besides my Lord Admiral and his two sons'. When at the Lord Admiral's intervention he was released, Stone praised him as a 'very *pitiful* Lord'. (*A Jacobean Journal*, p. 191.)

P. 43 L. 29 *A pestilent gall to me:* i.e., this pestilent fool rubs me sore.

P. 44 L. 4 *Learn more ... trowest:* hear more than you believe.

P. 44 L. 5 *Set less ... throwest:* don't bet a larger stake than you can afford to lose.

P. 44 L. 27 *motley:* the fool's parti-coloured uniform.

P. 45 L. 1 *monopoly:* a royal patent giving the holder sole right to deal in some commodity. The granting of these monopolies was one of the abuses of the age.

P. 45 L. 11 *like myself:* i.e. like a fool.

P. 45 L. 13 *Fools had ne'er ... apish:* i.e. there's no job left for fools now because the wise men are so like them.

P. 45 L. 24 *play bo-peep:* be a child again.

P. 46 L. 23 *which if you should ... discreet proceeding:* i.e., if you continue to be a nuisance I shall be forced to keep my state peaceful by means which usually would be shameful towards a father but would be justified as mere discretion.

P. 47 L. 7 *Whoop Jug I love thee:* Perhaps a refrain from a song.

P. 47 L. 32 *disquantity your train:* diminish the number of your followers.

P. 48 L. 21 *worships of their name:* i.e. behave with due regard to the honour of their names.

P. 48 L. 23 *like an engine:* like a little lever which can dislodge a fixed mass.

P. 48 L. 26 *Beat at this gate:* the first signs of madness.

P. 48 L. 32 *Hear Nature, hear:* Lear also calls on Nature, but as the goddess of natural affection.

P. 49 L. 13 *thankless child.* According to the accepted notion of the duties of children and parents, the child owed life (and therefore everything) to the parent.

P. 49 L. 20   *What fifty of my followers*: As Lear goes out he learns that Goneril has already herself taken steps to 'disquantity his train' by ordering that fifty shall depart within a fortnight.

P. 49 L. 24   *to shake my manhood*: i.e. with sobs.

P. 49 L. 28   *untented woundings*: raw wounds. A tent was a roll of lint used to clean out a wound before it was bandaged.

P. 50 L. 4   *resume the shape*: i.e. of King and tyrant.

P. 50 L. 23   *At point*: fully armed.

P. 51 L. 8   *compact it more*: make it stronger.

P. 51 L. 18   *Well, well, th' event*: we shall see what happens.

P. 52 L. 4   *kindly*: with the double meaning of 'dearly' and 'after her kind'.

P. 52 L. 15   *Canst tell how an oyster. ...* This well meaning but perpetual fretting by the fool is partly a cause of Lear's madness.

P. 53 L. 27   *queasy question*: i.e., which needs tender handling.

P. 54 L. 22   *conjuring the Moon*: invoking Hecate, goddess of witchcraft.

P. 55 L. 1   *in fine*: in short.

P. 55 L. 13   *arch and patron*: support and protector.

P. 55 L. 16   *to the stake*: so that he may be bound captive.

P. 56 L. 3   *All ports ... due note of him*: During the plots of 1603 and 1605 descriptions of the wanted men were broadcast by proclamation (which had not happened before for many years).

P. 56 L. 7   *natural*: here means 'loyal'.

P. 56 L. 8   *capable*: i.e. of succeeding to the Earldom.

P. 56 L. 26   *th' expense and waste of*: the spending of.

P. 57 L. 7   *fear'd of doing*: feared lest he do.

P. 58 L. 10   *Lipsbury pinfold*: this saying has not been explained. A pinfold is a village pound, a suitable place for a good fight whence neither party could escape.

P. 58 L. 15   Kent's abuse sums up the characteristics of the less reputable kind of gentleman-serving man or upstart courtier, hanging on to some great man. *Broken meats:* remains of food sent down from the high table; *worsted-stocking:* no gentleman, or he would have worn silk; *lily-livered:* white livered, cowardly;

P. 58 L. 24   *addition:* title.

P. 58 L. 31   *I'll make a sop o' th' moonshine of you:* Not satisfactorily explained, but obviously something unpleasant. Some critics say 'Knock you on your back in a puddle whence you'll look up at the moon'; others connect it with 'eggs in moonshine', a method of frying eggs; or perhaps Shakespeare simply means 'I'll make a wet mess of you.'

P. 59 L. 1   *barber-monger:* always in the barber's shop.

P. 59 L. 4   *Vanity the puppet:* Vanity appeared as an evil character in Morality Plays of the early 16th century, which still survived in a degenerate form in puppet shows exhibited at fairs.

P. 59 L. 23   *nature disclaims ... made thee:* i.e. You are no natural man, but only fine clothes.

P. 59 L. 33   *unnecessary letter:* because 'z' does not exist in Latin.

P. 60 L. 3   *wagtail:* an appropriate simile for a busy Court knave.

P. 60 L. 6   *anger ... privilege:* i.e., a man who has lost his temper may be allowed to raise his voice.

P. 60 L. 10   *holy cords ... t' unloose:* the bonds of affection (i.e. between husband and wife) too tightly bound to be unloosed.

P. 60 L. 14   *halcyon:* kingfisher. Kingfishers hung up by the neck were supposed always to turn their bills into the prevailing wind.

P. 60 L. 20   *cackling home to Camelot:* not yet explained. Camelot was Winchester, and the home of King Arthur and his Round Table.

P. 60 L. 27   *countenance ... me not:* I don't like his face.

P. 61 L. 1   *This is some fellow:* In plays of this time there was often depicted an outspoken servant or courtier, such as Thersites in *Troylus and Cressida* and Jaques in *As you Like It*, Macilente in Jonson's *Every Man out of his Humour*, or Marston's *Malcontent*. They existed also in real life. Henry Cuffe, the Earl of Essex's secretary, was a notable instance – 'a man of secret ambitious ends of his own, and of proportionate counsels sustained under the habit of a scholar, and slubbered over with a certain rude and clownish fashion, that had the semblance of integrity'. Cuffe was largely responsible for Essex's rebellion and death.

P. 61 L. 3   *constrains ... Nature*: affects a manner which is quite unnatural.

P. 61 L. 9   *silly ducking observants*: servants who watch obsequiously for their master's commands and are for ever bowing.

P. 61 L. 11   *Sir, in good faith*: Kent changes his tone from honest malcontent to affected courtier.

P. 61 L. 27   *a deal of man*: pretence of being a fine fellow.

P. 61 L. 33   *Ajax is their fool*: This cryptic but devastating remark moves Cornwall to fury, for by Kent's insolent tone and manner he realizes that by 'Ajax' he is himself intended. Kent implies that 'all these rogues and cowards are fooling this Ajax'. Ajax was the ridiculous braggart of the Greek army, whom Shakespeare had already dramatized in *Troylus and Cressida*. The name had further and unsavoury significances for the original audience for 'Ajax' was a common synonym for a jakes – a very evil smelling apartment. 'Ajax' therefore means 'a stinking braggart'.

P. 62 L. 24   *the King must take it ill*: To treat a King's messenger disrespectfully was an insult which, between reigning sovereigns, would have led to immediate war.

P. 63 L. 4   *rubb'd*: one of Shakespeare's many bowling metaphors; checked, as the bowl by uneven ground or another bowl.

P. 63 L. 14   *Heaven's benediction ... warm sun*: i.e., from the shade into the heat.

P. 63 L. 16   *beacon ... globe*: i.e., the rising sun.

P. 63 L. 18   *Nothing ... misery*: i.e., only the wretched can appreciate miracles.

P. 63 L. 27   *Enter Edgar.* The Folio (unlike modern editions) marks no change of scene for Edgar's brief appearance. On the Elizabethan stage none would be necessary, for Kent in the stocks at the back of the stage would not be noticed by Edgar in his passage from door to door across the front of the stage; see illustration p. 13.

P. 64 L. 1   *poorest shape ... beast:* poverty to show that man is a contemptible creature reduced to the level of a beast.

P. 64 L. 8   *Bedlam beggars:* see note on p. 37 l. 26.

P. 64 L. 26   *cruel:* with a pun on *crewel:* worsted.

P. 65 L. 11   *respect ... outrage:* such an insult to the respect due to a King.

P. 65 L. 18   *reeking post:* sweating messenger. In Shakespeare's time there was regular post service for official letters established on the main roads. At each stage horses were kept ready for the post-boy.

P. 65 L. 21   *spite of intermission:* although an interruption of my message.

P. 66 L. 2   *Fathers that wear rags:* children pretend to be blind when their fathers are in want.

P. 66 L. 7   *turns the key:* opens the door.

P. 66 L. 8   *dolours:* sorrows with an inevitable pun on 'dollars'.

P. 66 L. 10   *Oh how this mother ... below:* The *mother*, or *hysterica passio* is a form of suffocation, a feeling of 'the heart in the mouth', and the physical result of intense emotion.

P. 66 L. 23   *We'll set thee to school:* The fool, who is but a half-wit, is so triumphant at Kent's discomfiture, that he strings off a number of wise sayings to show his superiority.

P. 67 L. 33   *Infirmity ... bound:* When a man is sick he neglects his ordinary duty.

P. 68 L. 29   *I would divorce ... an adulteress:* i.e., would suspect that your dead mother was false to me.

P. 68 L. 32   *hath tied ... here:* i.e. at his heart.

P. 69 L. 14   *Nature ... confine:* your natural course of life is nearly finished.

P. 70 L. 13   *scant my sizes:* cut off my allowances.

P. 71 L. 9   *All's not ... terms so:* I do not necessarily offend because a silly old man says so.

P. 71 L. 12   *Will you yet hold:* i.e., because of the violent beating of his heart.

P. 72 L. 7   *imbossed carbuncle:* swollen boil.

P. 72 L. 18   *mingle reason with your passion:* consider your passion with reason.

P. 73 L. 21   *O reason ... need:* i.e., the needs of a beggar are very different from the needs of a King. *In the poorest thing superfluous:* even their few possessions are not absolutely necessary.

P. 74 L. 7   *No, I'll not weep:* In great mental distress Nature gives a man four degrees of relief: words, tears, madness, death. In cursing Goneril, Lear has exhausted the relief of words; he will not weep; a little more, and his sanity must crack.

P. 74 L. 17   *For his particular:* for himself alone.

P. 74 L. 33   *wilful men ... schoolmasters:* the headstrong must be taught by experience.

P. 75 L. 23   *little world of man:* It was a common Elizabethan idea, sometimes elaborately worked out, that man was a little universe (*microcosm*) and reproduced in himself the movements of the great universe (*macrocosm*).

P. 76 L. 2   *warrant of my note:* trusting you by what I have noted.

P. 77 L. 15   *drown'd the cocks:* i.e. the weathercocks.

P. 77 L. 22   *Court holy-water:* flattery of great men.

P. 78 L. 8   *The cod-piece ... wake:* The Fool's remarks, especially when deliberately cryptic, are always difficult to paraphrase. He means 'The man who goes wenching before he has a roof over his head will become a lousy beggar. The man who is kinder to his toe (i.e. his daughters) than to his heart (i.e. himself) will be kept awake by his troubles.' *cod-piece:* opening in front of the hose, indelicately conspicuous in masculine attire.

P. 78 L. 33   *pudder:* confusion; the Quarto reads 'pother'. As

Lear's wits begin to turn, he understands more clearly the mystery of things.

P. 79 L. 8 *Rive your concealing continents:* split open that which covers and conceals you.

P. 79 L. 9 *summoners:* the officers of the Ecclesiastical Court who summoned those guilty of immorality to appear.

P. 79 L. 22 *The art of our necessities … precious:* i.e., As the art of alchemy makes gold out of base metal, so our necessities make even straw a precious discovery.

P. 79 L. 33 *I'll speak a prophecy:* The fool in his catalogue of impossibilities parodies the rhyming and riddling prophecies popular at the time, which were attributed to 'Merlin' (the magician of King Arthur's Court), as later prophecies were attributed to 'Mother Shipton.'

P. 80 L. 15 *Merlin … his time:* Mock pedantry from Shakespeare, who was not usually careful about his historical sequence. Lear, according to the Chronicles, reigned some generations before King Arthur.

P. 81 L. 7 *forbid thee:* forbidden to thee.

P. 81 L. 25 *But where … felt:* the greatest malady is in my heart, so that I scarcely feel the outward suffering.

P. 81 L. 30 *tempest … beats there:* Lear is afflicted by the storm without and the storm of passion within, which is part mental, part physical, as the pulsations of his heart will not let him forget it.

P. 82 L. 17 *Poor naked wretches:* This is Lear's practical lesson in the meaning of poverty. *Loop'd and window'd,* i.e. full of holes.

P. 83 L. 4 *Didst thou … come to this:* i.e. nothing less than such sufferings could have reduced you to this misery. The sight of the bedlam is too much for Lear who now goes quite mad.

P. 83 L. 21 *he reserv'd a blanket:* The bedlam wore only a blanket (see p. 64 ll. 4–5).

P. 83 L. 31 *pelican daughters:* the pelican was regarded as the pattern of parental piety, for it fed its young on its own blood: Lear's unnatural daughters devour their parent.

P. 84 L. 8   *serving-man:* see p. 58 ll. 15–24 and p. 60 ll. 8–16.

P. 84 L. 19   *pen from lender's books:* a signed promise to pay was often recorded in the moneylender's ledger.

P. 84 L. 26   *Thou ow'st ... lendings.* Lear's ravings have usually a subtle sense. The bedlam, he says, has borrowed nothing from silkworm or beast: but he, Kent and the fool are sophisticated – i.e. adulterated, wearing garments not their own. He will therefore strip himself naked and be simple man.

P. 85 L. 21   *whipp'd ... imprison'd:* a rogue, according to the statute 39 Elizabeth, shall 'be stripped naked from the middle upwards, and shall be openly whipped until his or her body be bloody, and shall be forthwith sent from parish to parish by the officers of every the same the next straight way to the parish where he was born'.

P. 85 L. 27   *Smulkin ..., Modo, ... Mahu:* The bedlam is calling on his familiar spirits. Shakespeare took these names from Harsnett's *Egregious Popish Impostures* (see Introduction, p. 17).

P. 85 L. 33   *hate what gets it:* i.e. our children hate their parents.

P. 86 L. 11   *learned Theban:* i.e. Greek philosopher.

P. 85 L. 28   *cry you mercy, sir:* a common courtesy phrase as 'I beg your pardon'.

P. 87 L. 7   *good Athenian:* (as Theban above).

P. 88 L. 23   *whether a madman ... yeoman:* the fool is interested in the social status of a madman, and proceeds to argue the case.

P. 88 L. 27   *mad yeoman ... son a gentleman:* One of the social changes of the time much commented on. Many farmers who had become wealthy by war profits and enclosures sent their sons to London to learn to become gentlemen and to 'buy a coat from the heralds'. The process is illustrated in Jonson's *Every Man out of his Humour.*

P. 89 L. 6   *want'st thou eyes, at trial:* i.e., can't you see who is present at the trial – but Edgar is talking deliberate nonsense.

P. 89 L. 19   *robed man of justice:* i.e., with another glance at Edgar's blanket.

P. 89 L. 20   *yoke-fellow of equity:* fellow judge.

P. 89 L. 21   *o' th' commission:* Persons of high rank or charged with extraordinary crimes were not tried before the ordinary courts but by commissioners specially appointed.

P. 90 L. 24   *horn:* a horn bottle carried by beggars in which they collected the drink given by the charitable.

P. 91 L. 17   *This rest:* Lear can never have any rest for his tortured nerves.

P. 91 L. 22   *Exeunt:* the Fool is not seen again.

P. 91 L. 23   *When we ... fellowship:* when we see better men than ourselves suffering as we do, our sufferings seem slight. The man who suffers endures most in his mind as he contrasts the present misery with the happy past; but the mind suffers far less when it has companions in misery.

P. 91 L. 32   *Mark the high noises:* i.e., the 'hue and cry' of the pursuers.

P. 93 L. 5   *our power ... courtesy to our wrath:* i.e., 'we may gratify our anger by some punishment short of death which will pass for a loss of temper'.

P. 93 L. 20   *pluck me by the beard:* the greatest indignity that could be offered. Note how here and so often the stage directions for the action are all contained in the dialogue.

P. 93 L. 25   *hospitable favours:* the face of your host.

P. 94 L. 8   *charg'd at peril:* i.e. solemnly commanded. Solemn commands often included the phrase 'at peril of our displeasure'; it was a degree less formidable than 'on your allegiance' (p. 28 l. 15).

P. 94 L. 11   *stand the course:* i.e. like the bear in the bear-baiting pit I must endure a round.

P. 94 L. 22   *turn the key:* let them in.

P. 94 L. 23   *All cruels ... subscribe:* all other cruel things were on his side.

P. 96 L. 7   *old course of death:* natural death.

P. 96 L. 21   *The lowest ... yield to age:* i.e. when things are at the worst there is still hope, for there is nothing worse to fear; the worst change is from good to evil; a change from evil brings joy. After this poor comfort that nothing worse can happen to him, he sees his blinded father and continues, 'one would not trouble to live but to spite the hated world'.

P. 97 L. 10   *Full oft ... commodities:* often prosperity makes us careless (*secure*), and then our misfortunes prove blessings.

P. 97 L. 20   *the worst is not ... worst:* i.e. so long as a man is alive, he may yet reach a lower depth of misery.

P. 98 L. 1   *Bad is the trade ... others:* i.e., this pretending to be mad and so fooling a man in such distress as Gloucester, is now hateful.

P. 98 L. 11   *times' plague:* a sign of these diseased times.

P. 98 L. 19   *daub:* plaster it over, pretend.

P. 98 L. 27   *Obidicut ... Flibbertigibbet:* these names also come from Harsnett.

P. 98 L. 30   *mopping and mowing:* grinning and grimacing.

P. 99 L. 3   *Let the superfluous:* As Lear learns sense in his madness, so Gloucester sees clear in blindness. This passage echoes Lear's words (p. 82 l. 16).

P. 99 L. 4   *slaves your ordinance:* treats the will of Heaven like a slave, i.e., contemptuously.

P. 99 L. 6   *distribution ... excess:* the man with too much would distribute his wealth.

P. 99 L. 21   *my Lord:* Edmund is now Earl of Gloucester.

P. 100 L. 4   *tie him to an answer:* force him to retaliate.

P. 100 L. 5   *May prove effects:* may be fulfilled.

P. 100 L. 11   *mistress's command:* in all meanings of the word 'mistress'.

P. 100 L. 24   *worth the whistle:* The proverb runs ''Tis a poor dog that is not worth the whistle': so Goneril means 'I was once worth regarding as a dog'.

P. 100 L. 28   *That nature ... deadly use:* i.e., that creature which treats with scorn its origin (i.e. parent) cannot be kept within bounds: she that cuts herself off from her family tree, will perish and like a dead branch come to the burning.

P. 100 L. 33 *the text is foolish:* i.e. this is a silly sermon.

P. 101 L. 17 *honour ... suffering:* i.e., you cannot see that the insults which you suffer are dishonourable to you.

P. 101 L. 20 *noiseless:* i.e., unprepared.

P. 101 L. 25 *Proper deformity:* deformity proper to a fiend.

P. 101 L. 28 *self-cover'd:* i.e. hiding your true self (devil) under the guise of a woman.

P. 102 L. 1 *Marry ... mew:* you're a fine specimen of a man.

P. 102 L. 1 *Mew:* i.e. she makes a catcall.

P. 102 L. 9 *thrill'd with remorse:* trembling with pity.

P. 102 L. 24 *the building in my fancy:* 'my castle in the air,' i.e. of marrying Edmund.

P. 104 L. 1 *like a better way:* made her more lovely.

P. 104 L. 5 *Sorrow ... become it:* Sorrow would be much sought for, if it could make everyone so lovely.

P. 104 L. 15 *clamour moisten'd her:* her cries of grief drew forth tears.

P. 105 L. 22 *high-grown field:* i.e. the season is late summer.

P. 105 L. 29 *simples operative:* efficacious herbs.

P. 107 L. 17 *of her bosom:* familiar with her.

P. 107 L. 20 *take this note:* note this.

P. 107 L. 26 *desire her call her wisdom to her:* tell her not to be a fool.

P. 108 L. 18 *how fearful ... headlong:* This vivid description seems based on observation. The King's Players visited Dover in September 1606.

P. 109 L. 9 *Fairies, and Gods:* The story is pre-Christian, and so the characters call naturally upon the gods of the 'elder world'.

P. 109 L. 15 *Is done to cure it:* Edgar's purpose is to persuade his blinded father to go on living by the thought that he has been miraculously preserved. On a modern stage this episode is unconvincing: on the Elizabethan stage the scene probably opened on the gallery. While Gloucester is praying Edgar comes down from the gallery and reappears on the main stage as Gloucester falls from above (see illustration, p. 13.).

When he speaks again he has abandoned his lunatic mouthings and speaks as a normal man.

P. 109 L. 22   *snuff*: the smoking end of a burnt out candle.

P. 110 L. 16   *When misery ... proud will*: i.e. by suicide.

P. 110 L. 27   *whelk'd, and waved*: twisted and wavy.

P. 110 L. 29   *honours ... impossibilities*: caused themselves to be honoured by performing miracles.

P. 111 L. 4   *Enter Lear mad*: 'With poignant chances of recovery, no sooner discovered then destroyed, Lear passes into deeper insanity; his talk then leaps from one subject to another with wilder haste; and still there is a contexture in it. He has now the additional confusion of the rumoured war with France among his principal motives. And so, when he has made his escape at Dover, and comes with his crown of weeds to the side of Gloucester and Edgar, he begins: 'No, they cannot touch me for coining'; the metaphor echoes, and he changes it into actuality, 'There's your press-money'. He is 'the king himself', preparing his army for the quarrel with France, inspecting recruits. 'That fellow handles his bow like a crow-keeper.' Again we must see not only the fantasy of Lear, but the bird-boy passing over the farm. 'Look, look! a mouse'; apparently a reminiscence of the classical proverb, certainly a Falstaffian comment on a supposed recruit's usefulness, and clearly a remark brought on by his spying a field mouse in the corn. 'O! well flown, bird,' by no great extension of this, is his enthusiasm for falconry bursting forth as he sees a hawk drop on that mouse. We have from him a picture both of the country circumstances and his life and times. 'Give the word,' he finishes, like a sentry. 'Sweet marjoram,' says Edgar. It sounds 'aloof from the entire point'; yet Lear says 'Pass'. And with good secret reason. Sweet marjoram was accounted, according to Culpeper, a blessed remedy for diseases of the brain. Edgar was clearly a friend.' (Edmund Blunden. *Shakespeare's Significances*.)

P. 111 L. 30   *trick*: peculiar note.

P. 112 L. 8 *fitchew:* pole-cat, a creature most demonstratively eager at mating time. *soiled:* fed on spring grass.

P. 112 L. 11 *but to:* only down as far as.

P. 112 L. 22 *squiny:* glance sideways, like a prostitute.

P. 112 L. 22 *blind Cupid:* the sign over a brothel.

P. 112 L. 24 *all thy letters suns:* as large and bright as the sun.

P. 113 L. 4 *handy-dandy:* still used in the nursery: 'Handy-pandy, sugar candy, which hand will you have?'

P. 113 L. 13 *usurer … cozener:* i.e. the shady financier hangs the petty cheater.

P. 113 L. 23 *matter and impertinency:* sense and nonsense.

P. 113 L. 32 *a good block:* Lear's ravings have still a logical connection. The *block* is the shape and style of a felt hat, lit. the block on which it is moulded. *Hat* suggests felt, and that suggests muffling horse hoofs for a night surprise.

P. 114 L. 16 *I will die bravely, like a smug bridegroom:* It was said of Sir Charles Danvers, executed for his share in Essex's rebellion in 1600, that he was most cheerful at his end, 'rather like a bridegroom than a prisoner appointed for death'.

P. 114 L. 21 *sa, sa, sa, sa:* a cry sometimes used to indicate sudden action.

P. 115 L. 1 *main descry … thought:* the sight of the main body is hourly expected.

P. 116 L. 1 *Chill:* I'll. Edgar speaks stage rustic dialect.

P. 116 L. 6 *che vor' ye:* I warn yer.

P. 116 L. 28 *Leave:* i.e. by your leave – as he breaks the seal and opens the letter.

P. 116 L. 33 *will want not:* i.e. if desire (in all senses) is not lacking.

P. 117 L. 11 *Thee:* i.e. the corpse of Oswald. *post:* messenger.

P. 117 L. 14 *death-practis'd:* whose death is plotted.

P. 118 L. 4 *Be better suited:* i.e., abandon your disguise as a servant.

P. 118 L. 16 *wind up:* i.e., as a slack string of a musical instrument.

P. 118 L. 17 *child-changed:* so transformed by the cruelty of his children.

P. 121 L. 8   *Report is changeable:* rumours are not reliable.

P. 121 L. 13   *point and period:* lit. full stop, end.

P. 121 L. 22   *constant pleasure:* final decision.

P. 122 L. 14   *rigour of our state:* our harsh government.

P. 122 L. 16   *this business ... oppose:* this business affects particularly, because France is invading our country, not because he is encouraging the King and those other enemies who are rightfully opposed to us.

P. 124 L. 4   *for my state ... debate:* my fortunes are now in such a state that I must act, not argue.

P. 125 L. 5   *their greater pleasures:* the will of my superiors.

P. 125 L. 20   *take upon's the mystery of things:* pretend to understand deep policy.

P. 125 L. 29   *good-years:* a difficult phrase. Its origin apparently is in the phrase 'What the good-year', meaning much the same as 'What the hell'. Hence 'good-year' came to have some general meaning of evil beings, or bogey-men. Cordelia, in Lear's imagination, is once more his little girl and he talks baby language to her.

P. 127 L. 14   *immediacy ... your brother:* i.e. since he is *my* general, he is fit to be considered *your* equal.

P. 127 L. 28   *the walls is thine:* i.e., you have won the outward defences.

P. 128 L. 11   *An interlude:* i.e., this is mere play-acting.

P. 133 L. 5   *And there I left him tranc'd:* In the performance the significance of Edgar's speech can easily be missed: old Gloucester has already died of a broken heart; Kent too is near death.

P. 135 L. 29   *where is your servant Caius:* This is the first and only hint of a Caius – presumably the name assumed by Kent in his disguise. 'Is' should perhaps read 'was'. *O see, see:* There is a sudden change in Lear.

P. 136 L. 27   *undo this button:* for the last time Lear is oppressed by the violent throbbing of his heart before it is finally stilled.

✶

GLOSSARY

addition: title, honour.

admiration: affected wonder.

affected: shown affection for.

all-licensed: allowed to say any-
thing.

alteration: vacillation.

anatomise: dissect.

ancient of war: experienced in
war.

apish: imitative.

approves: confirms.

arbitrement: decision.

arch: chief support.

aroint: be off.

attaint: impeachment.

avert: turn.

ballow: cudgel.

bans: curses.

beguile: cheat.

bench: sit.

benison: blessing.

bewray: betray.

bias of nature: nature inclina-
tion.

biding: resting place.

blanket: cover with a blanket.

blown: puffed out.

bond: agreement, duty.

boot: advantage.

bourn: boundary.

brach: bitch.

brazed: become brazen.

breed occasions: find excuses.

cadent: falling.

canker-bit: corrupted by mag-
gots.

carbonado: piece of meat, slashed
for grilling.

carry it so: make it so appear.

casement: window.

century: company, a hundred
men.

champains riched: enriched by
fertile fields.

character: handwriting.

charge: expense.

choler: wrath.

chough: jackdaw.

clotpoll: blockhead.

cock: cock-boat, the ship's boat
which was towed behind.

common bosom: the sympathy of
the common people.

compact: made firmer, in league
with.

compeers: takes equal rank.

conceit: imagination.

conjunct: allied.

constant: firm.

contemn: despise.

corky: dry, withered

costard: lit. apple, head.

cowish: cowardly.

cozen'd: cheated.

crab: crab apple.

cross lightning: forked lightning.

crosses: troubles.

cub-drawn: sucked dry, and so hungry and ferocious.

cullionly: rascally.

curiosity: 1. niceness; 2. exactness.

curst: sharp, bitter.

dear: important.

debosh'd: debauched.

defuse: make indistinct.

depositories: trustees.

derogate: debased.

difference: quarrel.

disnatur'd: unnatural.

distract: mad.

ditch-dog: dog drowned in a ditch.

doubted: feared.

ear-kissing: whispered close.

elf: tangle.

epicurism: self-indulgence.

evasion: excuse.

even o'er: go over.

eyeless: blind.

faint neglect: suspicion of neglect.

fastened: hardened.

fear judgment: respect the law.

fell: fierce.

festinate: speedy.

fetches: excuses.

flaws: pieces.

fleshment: excitement.

foins: fencing thrusts.

fond: foolish.

footed: on the move.

fordid: destroyed.

fore-vouch'd: previously declared.

for-fended: forbidden.

fork: two-pointed arrow.

fraught: laden, endowed.

fret: wear away.

frontlet: forehead, frown.

furnishings: outward trappings.

gallow: terrify.

gasted: frightened.

generous: noble.

germens: seeds of life.

glass eyes: spectacles.

goest: i.e., on foot.

got: begot.

graced: gracious, honourable.

half-blooded: bastard.

hatch: half door.

head-lugged: born by dogs in baiting.

Hecate: goddess of night and witchcraft.

high-engendered: joined on high, in the sky.

hospitable favours: features of your host.

images: signs.

impatience: suffering.

important: importunate.

impress'd lances: conscript soldiers.

ingenious: sensitive.

intelligent party: intelligence agent.

interess'd: interested.

invention: plan.

it: its.

iakes: latrine.

kibes: blisters.

knapp'd: cracked.

latch'd: wounded.

lag: lagging behind, i.e., younger.

lethargied: paralyzed.

luxury: lust.

lym: bloodhound.

machinations: plotting.

maugre: in spite of.

meads: pasture lands.

meiny: company.

minikin: dainty.

mo: more.

monsters: makes monstrous.

nether stocks: stockings.

nicely: with a nice regard for formality.

nighted: darkened.

nine-fold: with nine evil spirits.

nursery: care.

œillades: loving looks.

opposite: opponent.

orbs: stars.

out-wall: outward appearance.

overture: disclosure.

owes: owns.

packs and sects: factions and parties.

pain: labour.

'parel: apparel.

pass: pass sentence.

pelting: paltry.

perdu: sentry in an exposed position.

period: end.

pieced: add to.

pight: pledged.

placket: opening in the petticoat.

plate: protect.

poise: weight.

power: army.

practice: plot.

prefer : promote.

pregnant : able to conceive.

presently : immediately.

pressed : immediate.

prevented : forestalled.

proof and preachment : example.

propinquity : relationship.

put it on : encourage.

qualified : mixed, moderate.

question : come to life.

questrists : searchers.

quit : requite, defend.

razed : erased, disguised.

remember'st : remindest.

remorse : pity.

repeal : recall from banishment.

respect : regard for.

reverb : echo.

sallets : salads.

saw : proverb.

scanted : curtailed.

scattered : disunited.

seconds : supports.

sectary astronomical : follower of the sect of astronomers.

seeming : hypocrisy.

sequent : subsequent.

several : separate.

shealed peascod : pod without the peas.

simples operative : effective remedies.

simular : pretended.

smilets : little smiles.

snuffs and packings : offences and plots.

sovereign : ruling, predominant.

spleen : malice.

star-blasting : evil caused by the stars.

stelled fires : light of the stars.

still : always.

still-soliciting : always asking for something.

stomach : anger.

strained : excessive.

strangered : made a stranger.

sub-contracted : already bespoke.

subscription : allegiance.

sumpter : baggage animal.

superfluous : having too much.

tax : censure.

teem : breed.

temper : mix.

temperance : sanity.

tender : offer.

tender-hefted : delicately-framed.

thought-executing : killing as quick as thought.

top : head.

trowest : knowest.

trundle-tail : curly tail.

unbolted : unsifted.

undistinguished : limitless.

vent : utter.

wakes: merry makings.
wants: lacks.
washed: weeping.
web and pin: eye diseases.
weeds: garments.
well-favoured: sleek.

white herring: pickled herring.
wide-skirted: extensive.
will: 1. intention; 2. purpose;
   3. lust.
wind me: insinuate.
worth: worthy.

*